Praise for
The Kingdom Series

"Quite simply, the Kingdom Series is brilliant. Chuck's allegorical tales have provided a fresh light with which to illuminate biblical narratives, and because of his words, I have been left challenged, encouraged, and enlightened."
—LINDSAY, age 23

"I cannot wait until I can buy the last three of the series! Your books really inspire me to fight for the King and have helped me to grow closer to God. I cannot thank you enough for that. The King reigns—and His Son!"
—ETHAN, age 11

"These are my absolute favorite books. They are filled with non-stop action, adventure, and the Word of the Lord all in one. My friends love the books too!"
—KELSEY, age 13

"The Kingdom Series is a wonderful way to introduce discussions of the end times, as well as to encourage us to be ready servants and prepared knights for our King. On a spiritual level and on an allegorically literary level, this is an outstanding series of books to consider."
—KRIS, The Book Peddler

"This is an awesome product with great appeal without involving the use of 'magic.' This series inspires believers to fulfill their call and opened up great discussions with our home-schooling group. My son kept asking for more, so we also read it aloud as a family, and it made for many pleasant evenings snuggling on the couch reading together!"
—JULIE

Look for other books in the Kingdom Series:

Kingdom's Dawn (Book One)
Kingdom's Hope (Book Two)
Kingdom's Edge (Book Three)
Kingdom's Call (Book Four)
Kingdom's Reign (Book Six)

THE KINGDOM SERIES

BOOK 5

KINGDOM'S QUEST

CHUCK BLACK

MULTNOMAH

KINGDOM'S QUEST

All Scripture quotations and paraphrases are taken from the New King James Version®. Copyright © 1982 by Thomas Nelson Inc. Used by permission. All rights reserved.

Trade Paperback ISBN 978-1-59052-749-8
eBook ISBN 978-0-307-56186-2

"Ballad of the Prince" music and lyrics copyright © 2006 by
Emily Elizabeth Black

Illustrations by Marcella Johnson, copyright © 2006 Perfect Praise Publishing

Published in association with The Steve Laube Agency, LLC, 5501 North Seventh Avenue, #502, Phoenix, AZ 85013

Published in the United States by Multnomah, an imprint of the Crown Publishing Group, a division of Penguin Random House LLC, New York.

MULTNOMAH® and its mountain colophon are registered trademarks of Penguin Random House LLC.

Library of Congress Cataloging-in-Publication Data
Black, Chuck.
    Kingdom's quest / Chuck Black. — 1st ed.
        p. cm. — (The kingdom series ; bk. 5)
    ISBN 978-1-59052-749-8
    I. Title.
PS3602.L264K573 2007
813'.6—dc22.

2007000509

Printed in the United States of America
2020

20 19 18 17 16

To the future generations of saints.
May you boldly take up your sword
and follow Jesus!

CONTENTS

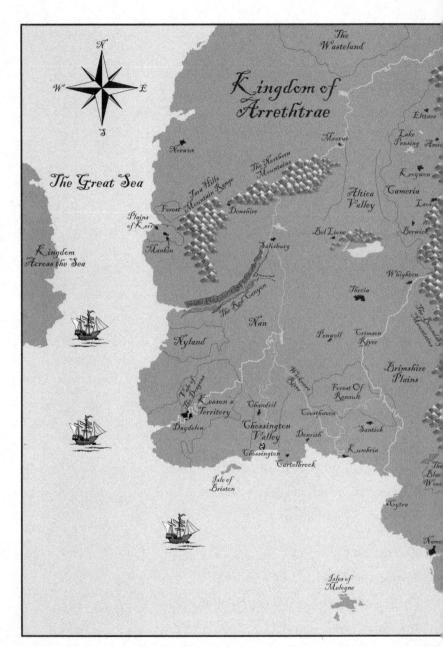

© Chuck Black

BASTION
OF EVIL

I am Cedric of Chessington, Knight of the Prince and humble servant of the same. I have heard the tales of a hundred mighty men and seen the flashing blades of a thousand more. Though I am wholly undeserving of the favor of the King and His noble Son, here I sit, ready to fight for the Prince against the approaching evil forces of the Dark Knight and his Shadow Warriors. I am not worthy, but the Prince has made me so, for He lifted me from the depths of peasantry and made me a son…a knight to carry the brilliant sword of His Code and the truth of His sacrifice for the people to the far reaches of the kingdom. In your corner of the kingdom, I can only hope that the feeble words of my story might light upon your ears and bring understanding of the great significance of the majestic Prince and His mission to save the people.

Perhaps you have joined me in times past to hear the story of one much greater than I…the gallant Sir Gavinaugh. From my heart I tell the truth—no mortal man born in Arrethtrae has served the King and the Prince with more zeal than he. As a persecutor of the Knights of the Prince, his remarkable encounter with the Prince Himself transformed his passionate course of destruction into a beacon of light that burned brighter than the fires in the caverns of Sedah. My time of service to the

Prince in the coming great battle is near, but the tale of the gallant Sir Gavinaugh must be told, for his work in this land was powerful and his influence great. He was trained and knighted near the Crimson River by the Prince Himself.

He faced a kingdom of enemies and skeptics, but his passion was not hindered, for the power of the Prince was strong in his heart, and his sword was now the sword of truth and justice. His was a quest to save a kingdom in chaos—a quest like no other! 🔷

CHAPTER ONE

A KNIGHT'S RETURN

Gavinaugh looked across the Brimshire Plains to the Boundary Mountains. He then turned and scanned northward toward Cameria, and finally west to the Forest of Renault and beyond where the Chessington Valley, Kesson's Territory, and the Great Sea lay. All he had really known was the city of Chessington and the surrounding regions, but his mind was slowly awakening to the enormity of the kingdom and his mission to reach all lands and all people with the story of the Prince.

Gavinaugh filled his lungs with the sweet, crisp morning air of the country and felt small. He slowly shook his head.

"You are troubled," the Prince said as He stood before Gavinaugh, ready to mount His steed.

"I am but one, my Lord, and I ache to reach all of Arrethtrae. I worry that my legs might not endure and the days of my life might not be numerous enough to reach them all. Where do I start?" He looked upon the royal face of the Prince.

The Prince smiled. "You start and end with Me, Gavinaugh. You are responsible for your service to Me, not for the decisions of others. Fulfill your duty one day at a time, and leave the outcome in My hands."

Gavinaugh understood and nodded.

"Your fellow knights do not trust you. Your journey to the ends of the kingdom must first pass through Chessington. They need to know that you are truly a Knight of the Prince."

"Yes, my Lord. But how am I to travel—"

The Prince held up His hand to silence him.

Gavinaugh knew that the Prince could hear something he could not. He strained to listen. A moment later he not only heard the rumble but felt the pounding in the earth of hundreds of horses. Out of the north he saw the growing mass of a mighty army approaching. He felt a swell of anxiety in his stomach and began to draw his sword.

"They are Mine," the Prince said as He mounted His steed.

He looked down at Gavinaugh, and in that moment Gavinaugh felt the gaze of a King upon him. Soon an army of mighty warriors enveloped them. They saluted the Prince and waited in silence for His command. The Prince's horse reared, and He led the force southward to the Great Sea. As the massive steeds and their riders passed by on each side, Gavinaugh recognized one warrior among them. Porunth broke off from the rest and came to him.

"You look well, my friend." Porunth smiled as he spoke above the thundering sound. The last of the warriors passed like a rush of wind, and the sound of beating hooves quickly diminished.

"I am well… Finally, I am well." Gavinaugh returned the smile.

Porunth nodded. "You have partaken of the character of the Prince. It is easy to tell when one has been with Him."

"I am humbly grateful and a privileged man."

"As are we all." Porunth looked toward his retreating force. "May your travels be fair and your battles sure, Sir Gavinaugh."

"And yours, good sir," Gavinaugh said. "You don't perhaps have an extra horse about, do you?"

"Strange you should ask," Porunth said. "You are not the only one who has skirted death." He smiled again and bolted away toward his army without another word.

Gavinaugh was confused, but he was learning that the messages of the Silent Warriors were oftentimes more like riddles. He watched the Prince's army diminish in the distance.

"I guess my travels will begin on foot," he said aloud and looked toward the forest from which he had come weeks earlier.

Just then a horse neighed loudly a short distance behind him, and Gavinaugh nearly jumped out of his armor. He turned to see a sight that delighted his soul.

"Triumph?"

He ran to the horse and could hardly contain his joy. "Triumph…it is you! How can this possibly be?"

Triumph seemed pleased to see Gavinaugh as well. He stroked the horse's neck and felt as though they were once again a team. In examining the horse, he noticed the scar on Triumph's shoulder, but otherwise he seemed healthy and whole.

He mounted Triumph and looked forward to his course back home.

After many days of traveling, Gavinaugh arrived in the Chessington Valley. He timed his arrival at dusk, for he was unsure of the status of the city and of the Noble Knights. He knew he must face Kifus one day, but now was not the time, for such an encounter would only hinder his call to the greater purpose of life.

He took the back alleyways to the home of a man named Tarill. He dismounted and knocked quietly at the back door, as he had done many times before. The door opened slightly, and a stout-looking man with a scraggly beard peered out.

"What in the…" The man opened the door to allow Gavinaugh entrance and then looked outside after him to confirm that no one was watching. He quickly closed and locked the door and turned to face Gavinaugh. This was no joyous reunion.

"I heard you were dead…or worse," Tarill said bluntly.

Gavinaugh did not respond. He produced a small bag that jingled with coins. "Where do they meet now?"

Tarill laughed. "So you've come to finish the job you started, eh? I guess I know which rumors to believe."

Gavinaugh was becoming uncomfortable, for here in the home of his old informant he was dramatically facing the reality of his former life.

"Just tell me the location, and I'll be on my way."

"Double the fee, and I will hand their leaders to you on a silver platter!" Tarill seemed thrilled with the prospect.

"How so?"

"An acquaintance of mine has gained the trust of two of their leaders, Barrett and William. He told me that there is a meeting arranged with one of the Followers from an Outdweller haven. With a little persuasion I can convince him to tell me the location. You and your men could take them with ease."

Gavinaugh thought for a moment and realized that this would be his best opportunity to reach the Knights of the Prince.

"Very well. I will agree on one condition. No one else, not even the Noble Knights, are to be told. Is that clear?"

Tarill's eyes narrowed. "All right, I can agree to that. What have you got up your sleeve, Gavin?"

Gavinaugh looked at the man fiercely. "If you betray me, Tarill, my next hunt will be for you."

Gavinaugh paid the man and left.

Two nights later, Gavinaugh cautiously approached a shop in the northern part of Chessington. He found an alcove and watched from the shadows of the night. The air was thick and still. He spotted the door that led to the chamber where the meeting was to be. The sounds of a city settling down for the night mixed with the chirp of crickets and an occasional barking hound. He was apprehensive, for he was not completely confident that Tarill could be trusted. He was a man who made his living on deception and on bartering one deal for another. Loyalty was not part of his character. Even if Tarill chose not to betray him, Gavinaugh wasn't sure how the Knights of the Prince would respond to him. Although he carried his sword, he knew that he could never draw it upon a fellow Knight of the Prince, even if it meant the end of his life.

After a long wait, Gavinaugh was fairly confident that no one was nearby. He walked to the door. He looked up and down the alley one more time, took a deep breath, then opened the door and stepped inside.

As he closed the door, his back was to the room.

"Finally, you've arrived," a man said.

Gavinaugh turned and faced the men.

"Were you delayed, Sir—"

Before him stood two men in tunics bearing the mark of the Prince. One was a bit shorter and nearly bald. Gavinaugh immediately recognized the taller, dark-haired knight as one of the first men he captured a long time ago. Gavinaugh had questioned him in the cells of the prison. The recognition was mutual, as evidenced by the look of shock on the man's face.

Both men immediately drew their swords and looked to the doors of the shop, apparently expecting a full ambush to crush down upon them.

Gavinaugh held up his hand. "I am alone, gentlemen. Please do not be alarmed."

The tension in the room was thick. Both men were poised in a fight-ready stance. Gavinaugh wondered if they would run him through and flee, but they did not attack.

The shorter man slowly moved to the front door.

"Check the street," the taller man said.

The other man opened the door a crack. "Two Noble Knights!" he said in a hushed tone.

"They are not with me. I didn't come to fight you. Please believe me," Gavinaugh said.

The two men gripped their swords tighter and took a step toward Gavinaugh.

"You are Sir Gavin, the Tyrant of Chessington. Why should we believe you?" the taller man said as he pointed his sword at him.

Just then the door behind Gavinaugh began to open, and dread filled his heart.

Tarill must have betrayed me! He turned toward the door and drew his sword. Only then did he realize his error. He was in the presence of men who regarded him as an enemy. With his sword in his hand, their perception was undeniable.

"It's a trick!" the shorter man exclaimed.

As they rushed upon Gavinaugh, he turned to face them and lowered his sword. The two men brought their swords back to strike. For a moment Gavinaugh wondered if his mission would be over before it began, but they did not finish their attack. It seemed to Gavinaugh as though they could not attack one who would not defend himself.

"We are among friends, gentlemen. Please lower your swords," a familiar voice said from behind Gavinaugh.

A Knight of the Prince entered and stood among the odd trio. The tension in the room abated somewhat.

"Weston, this is Gavin, the Noble Knight. He is here to either kill or capture us!"

"No, Sir William. I can assure you that he is not here for that," Weston replied.

The two men were clearly struggling with seeing Gavinaugh as anything but a ruthless persecutor of the Followers of the Prince. They did not lower their swords.

Weston walked between his friends and Gavinaugh. He turned his back to Gavinaugh and opened his arms to the two knights. Now their swords were pointed at Weston's chest.

"He is a fellow Knight of the Prince. I give you my life as my word."

They lowered their swords but did not appear convinced. Gavinaugh sheathed his sword.

"Barrett, check the door again," William said.

"All clear," Barrett replied.

Weston turned to face Gavinaugh, and the two embraced. "It is good to see you again, my friend."

"And you," he replied. "Your timing is impeccable."

"Sir William, Sir Barrett, meet Sir Gavinaugh of Chessington," Weston said.

With a sober heart, Gavinaugh spoke. "I have caused you and many others great suffering, and for that I am truly sorry. Were it not for the transforming power of the Prince, I would not be standing before you this evening. Please know that my heart beats with the sole purpose of proclaiming the Prince as the true Son of the King. I join my sword and my life to yours in this great mission."

Gavinaugh extended his left hand. William hesitated and then took it.

"The ways of the Prince are for everyone, even for one such as you," William said, and Gavinaugh remembered William speaking those words from long ago when he thought William to be a crazy man.

Barrett also accepted Gavinaugh's hand.

"I am no longer Gavin of Chessington, but Gavinaugh of Arrethtrae, for the Prince has made all things new in me. I apologize for the abrupt meeting, good sirs. My association with the Knights of the Prince is rather limited at this time, and I had no other way to contact you."

Barrett sheathed his sword. "Your disappearance was a great mystery to many in the city. We would love to hear your story."

Gavinaugh smiled and knew in his heart that this was the first of many opportunities he would have to share his story.

"I have been with the Prince…" As Gavinaugh told all to William and Barrett, his zeal for the Prince spilled into every word that came from his lips, and soon the men had become his loyal brothers as well.

"We must take you to Cedric. He will want to know of the great work the Prince has done in you," William said. "Weston, bring Gavinaugh to the haven tomorrow evening, and we will prepare Cedric and the others for his visit."

William turned to Gavinaugh. "We hope your next encounter with the Knights of the Prince will not be quite as intense."

Gavinaugh laughed. "Indeed!"

CHAPTER TWO

A JOURNEY
OF WILL

The meeting with Cedric and the other Knights of the Prince was at first cautious, then joyful, then exciting, as all became aware of the mighty work the Prince was beginning. Initially, some of the knights fell into dispute regarding the Outdwellers, arguing that they must first be made citizens of Chessington and prove that they would uphold the Articles of the Code. But Cedric stood with Gavinaugh as he declared the words of the Prince and His intention to make knights of Outdwellers, regardless of their citizenship. In the end, the hearts of all were unified and confirmed, for they accepted and understood the Prince's intention to reach the entire kingdom.

At the counsel of the Knights of the Prince, it was determined that Weston should travel with Gavinaugh for a time on his journeys to other cities and regions. They departed the following morning to the port city of Kumbria.

Kumbria was a quaint city nestled between the lush, rolling hills of the country and the shore of the Great Sea. It was an access point for much of the trade from other coastal regions to the eastern kingdom. Ships of all sizes and origins dotted the harbor of the city. Gavinaugh and Weston found a few people who were willing to hear their words from the Prince, but they perceived a strange fearfulness in the hearts of most. Ten came to believe on the Prince, and Gavinaugh and Weston began to train them diligently in the art of the sword to become true Knights of the Prince. Remarkably, they met no resistance, for there were no other knightly orders to take offense at their training.

One day while Gavinaugh and Weston were in the market square, a man approached Gavinaugh and spoke quietly, as though he did not want to be overheard. He glanced about the square as if searching for something or someone.

"What can I do for you, sir?" Gavinaugh asked.

"The prefect Sergustine of Kumbria wishes to meet with you," the man said, continuing the search with his eyes.

"We would be honored," Gavinaugh replied. "We will come with you now."

"No!" the man said quickly. "He will meet you at his manor in the back courtyard tomorrow morning at sunrise."

"We will be there," Gavinaugh said, and the nervous man departed at once.

Weston scratched his head. "What is it about this city?" Gavinaugh asked him.

"I don't know," Weston said. "The wealthy are certainly apprehensive, and I sense that our presence is becoming uncomfortable to them. Perhaps our recruits can give us an answer."

That evening Gavinaugh spoke with a young man named Cade. He said he had been drawn to Gavinaugh and Weston earlier while hearing them talk in the marketplace. He was curious about the strange story of the Prince and the order of the Knights of the Prince. Gavinaugh spoke with him while Weston worked with the other men.

"But I thought a man must possess great wealth and train many years in order to become a knight," Cade said.

Gavinaugh shook his head. "When a man's heart beats with the purpose of the Code and he follows the truth of the Prince, he is more of a knight than one who owns great lands and has trained with a sword since childhood. The ways of the Prince are a great mystery to those who don't believe, but to those of us who do, they are life itself. The irony is that the Prince calls the poor and the lowly, and not many wealthy or mighty will accept these truths and yield to Him. For a short time they will have their reward, but your reward is so much greater and will last forever. A grand manor awaits you in the Kingdom Across the Sea. Your reward will not ever be taken from you—not here or in the kingdom to come. We have become like the Prince Himself—joint heirs to the kingdom—and we will rule with Him one day."

"How can this be true? I am so unworthy...I am just a pauper." Cade seemed quite perplexed by Gavinaugh's words.

"Those who know they are unworthy and yet believe are true Knights of the Prince, for it was the death of the Prince that made them worthy. Those who think themselves worthy by their own skill and power shall never see the King's kingdom. It is only through His Son that one can find the way—the only way!"

Cade's face shone with interest. "What of the other knightly orders? They seem to uphold many of the same ideals as the Code of the King."

"Do not be deceived, young Cade. Only one order is the true order. Many are beguiled by the apparent goodness of the other orders, but they do not believe in the Prince or in His sacrificial mission to Arrethtrae. In reality, the Dark Knight is the architect behind these orders to entice as many away from the Prince as possible. He is as cunning as a serpent that has mesmerized its next victim. The ways of these orders seem right to many, but in the end, they will be destroyed."

"What of those who live by the true Code of the King? Are they worthy?"

"No man save One has perfectly fulfilled all of the Articles of the Code, and that man is the Prince. If a man believes he is worthy as a knight because he has fulfilled the Code, he is a liar and fools not only others but also himself. It is the Code that brings understanding to our unworthiness. Only when one accepts the truth of the Prince and His mission here in Arrethtrae is he worthy to become a Knight of the Prince. He cannot fulfill the Code, but nevertheless he is worthy because of the Prince alone."

"Do we then not live by the Code if we are unable to fulfill it?" Cade asked.

"May the King forbid it!" Gavinaugh said. "Because of the Prince, we are made worthy and we establish the Code all the more, for our hearts desire the ways of the Prince and to become like Him who fulfilled the Code to perfection."

"To believe in the Prince…it seems too simple, Sir Gavinaugh."

Gavinaugh smiled. "It is the simplest and the hardest thing you will ever do."

"Why do you say it is hard as well?"

"You must understand that if you become a Knight of the Prince and live by the Code, you will encounter great adversity. There are those who have left the order because of such challenges. The Prince requires complete surrender of all that you have and all that you are *to Him*. This is why the wealthy and the mighty find it nearly impossible to yield to Him. He must become their Lord, and often their pride and greed prevent it. When you become a Knight of the Prince, you join an order that is contrary to the rest of the kingdom, and you then become the adversary of the greatest enemy of the King that has ever existed— the Dark Knight and his Shadow Warriors. If you choose to follow the Prince, you must prepare yourself for great battles, young Cade. But remember that the Prince has promised that He will always, *always* be with you!"

Gavinaugh could see the light of truth twinkling in the young man's eyes.

"Are you prepared to take up the sword of the Prince? To give Him all that you have and all that you are? To honor and serve Him in all that you do? To endure the adversity that will surely come to you as one of His knights?"

"I am!" Cade answered.

"Kneel."

Cade reverently dropped to his knees.

"Do you believe in the Prince, the King's Son, and in His death on the tree to save you? Do you believe that He rose up from death and lives?"

"I do," Cade answered.

"Will you take up the sword of the Prince and uphold the King's Code unto your last breath?"

"I will."

Gavinaugh unsheathed his sword and touched Cade's shoulders with it as he spoke. "Then I dub you Sir Cade, Knight of the Prince! Rise, Sir Cade."

Cade stood, and his eyes gleamed with the light of his new life.

"All my life I have hoped to hear such words and thought them possible only in the words of a fairy tale. But here today I have been lifted from a life of despair and hopelessness into a life of promise and expectation. Now my life has purpose and meaning. I feel like a new man."

Gavinaugh placed a hand on his shoulder. "And that you are! Now you can help me discover some truth."

"What could I possibly teach you, Sir Gavinaugh?"

"Tell me about Prefect Sergustine."

"I don't know very much about him, but he seems to be an honest man," Cade said.

"Our presence here seems to have made the leaders of the city nervous. Do you have any idea why?" Gavinaugh asked.

"You are probably right, but they always seem nervous to me." Cade hesitated. "I only know of rumors as to why."

Gavinaugh looked into his eyes. "I am meeting with the prefect tomorrow. Perhaps your rumors will prepare me."

Cade hesitated and then nodded. "As a child, I once heard of a mysterious dark warrior who visited the prefect years ago. It is believed by some that he is the true prefect of the city and that Sergustine is simply a pawn used to bring the wealth of the city to the mysterious warrior. Some claim that this dark warrior lives nearby, but most everyone thinks him to be a myth. No one will speak of such things openly, though."

"Why not?" Gavinaugh asked.

"I'm sure it is just a coincidence, but a mischievous lad who claimed he saw this mysterious warrior one evening was found dead a couple of days after telling his story. People said he was kicked in the head by a horse, but some suspect that his untimely death was not an accident at all. I think perhaps your presence and talk of the Prince has resurrected this great superstition among the people. You should be careful, Sir Gavinaugh."

"This all sounds quite bizarre, but rest assured…I will be careful," Gavinaugh said.

That evening, Gavinaugh pondered all that Cade had said. There was indeed a strange and fearful heart among the citizens of Kumbria. It was a fear he had tasted once before.

CHAPTER THREE

BLACKNESS
OF A SHADOW

At sunrise the next morning, Weston and Gavinaugh rode to the prefect's manor. They left their horses to graze in a field nearby and walked to the courtyard at the back of his estate. The courtyard was large and beautiful, full of flowering trees and shrubbery that was manicured to perfection. It seemed more like a garden than a courtyard. Many cobblestone paths branched off of the main walkway that led to the manor, each one inviting a passerby to partake in the beauty.

The cool morning air was crisp, and the full light of the day was not yet upon them. The morning dew became a mist under the warmth of the coming day and rose from the greenery to place them as obscure figures on the canvas of a piece of masterful art. Just ahead, a man was pacing back and forth near a stone bench off the main walkway. Gavinaugh assumed that this was the prefect. At their approach, he looked up and beckoned them to come. They were still some distance away when the peace of the courtyard was shattered by the presence of evil.

A huge, ominous form stepped from the shadows of the nearby shrubbery onto the walkway between them and the prefect. His sword was drawn, and Gavinaugh instantly recognized the mark of Lucius on his armor. The prefect gasped and turned white. Gavinaugh could tell he wanted to run but did not dare. A branch as thick as a man's arm hung in front of the warrior, obscuring some of his form. The warrior growled and made one powerful slice with his sword that cut the branch clean through, exposing all his horrific grandeur to Gavinaugh and Weston. The warrior turned and pointed his sword at the prefect.

"You fool, Sergustine! Did you really think I wouldn't know?"

The prefect cowered in fear and became like stone. Gavinaugh sensed the fear rising in Weston, for he had never seen a Shadow Warrior before. Gavinaugh fought back his own apprehension—his previous encounters with such brutes had been devastating. But then he remembered the words of the Prince: *"Not even the forces of the Dark Knight will prevail against you!"*

Gavinaugh spoke in hushed tones to his comrade. "Do not fear, Weston. The Prince is with us."

The Shadow Warrior turned back to face them as Gavinaugh and Weston drew their swords. "This city belongs to me. I know who you are and why you are here. Leave now or I will kill you and hang your bodies in the city streets for all to see!" The Shadow Warrior's raspy voice was an unnatural sound in such a naturally beautiful place.

Gavinaugh felt a surge of strength pulse through his muscles as he brought the power of the Prince to the forefront of his mind. A burning indignation ignited his soul at the presence of the evil before him. He set his eyes upon the warrior and did not hesitate as he stepped forward with the confidence of one who knows that his life is in the hands of a Man a thousand times more powerful than the warrior before him.

Gavinaugh spoke as he approached. "Hear this, warrior of the Dark Knight. You are an enemy of good, and you pervert the ways of the King. By the power of the Prince, you shall be destroyed!"

The warrior was momentarily stunned by such a reply, and the wrath manifested in his face faltered.

Weston followed Gavinaugh, but the pathway was too narrow to stand beside him. Gavinaugh rushed upon the warrior, and a clash of steel resounded throughout the courtyard. The warrior recovered his fury and unleashed a volley of wild cuts and slices on Gavinaugh, but the skill of Gavinaugh's training did not waver. He deflected the blows with perfection and felt the rush of power in his blade like he had never felt in any other battle. Within a few moments, Gavinaugh knew the movements of the warrior so thoroughly that his steel arrived in a defensive position before the Shadow Warrior could finish a cut.

Gavinaugh predicted the brute's next attack, deflected it, and spun full circle with his sword so quickly that the Shadow Warrior did not even see the deadly slice that cut through his torso and ended his life.

The dark warrior collapsed on the cobblestones with a thud. Weston had circled behind the Shadow Warrior to protect the prefect, but by the time he had maneuvered into position, the fight was over.

Weston and Gavinaugh approached the prefect, who had not moved and was still stunned by what he had just seen. When they stood before him, the man fell to his knees and grabbed Gavinaugh's feet.

"You have saved me…you have saved us all! We shall be your servants forever!"

Gavinaugh knelt to lift the prefect by his arm. "Prefect, stand up. We have not saved you. The Prince has done this thing. Serve Him and Him only!"

The prefect stood and looked at Gavinaugh. "I heard of your visit to our city and the words you were speaking. I hardly dared to call you here, for I feared for my life, but I was a living dead man anyway. Tell me of the Prince that I might believe!"

The prefect brought Gavinaugh and Weston into his manor and gathered his servants and other city leaders to hear their words. From that day forth, the city of Kumbria became a strong haven of the Knights of the Prince…a beacon of light in the whole region. They remained many days with the people and trained hundreds of men and women in the ways of the Code and with the sword of the Prince, knighting all who believed and were willing to follow.

After many days, Gavinaugh and Weston departed from Kumbria with a promise to return and a charge to continue the work they had begun. They followed the coastal roadway for a time and then set their path toward the city of Santiok. They had heard that the people there were devoid of hope, for a prime commodity of the city was the souls of men and women, which brought gain to many and pain to many more. 🔲

CHAPTER FOUR

CHAINS
OF DESPAIR

Gavinaugh and Weston entered Santiok in midafternoon. It was a large city that was a hub for merchandise and trade in the region. Near the center of the city, a mass of people had gathered for a slave auction in progress. In this region of the kingdom, such barbaric practices were common. The slaves were taken from all regions of the land, and Santiok had become the center of the slave trade. Gavinaugh and Weston were aware of this, but experiencing the culture firsthand was demoralizing.

As they approached the auction platform, Gavinaugh and Weston could hear the voices of crude men bartering for human lives, and Gavinaugh felt the anger rise within him.

Weston grabbed Gavinaugh's arm. "Remember, Gavinaugh, they do not know the ways of the Prince. They have lived in this darkened condition since the beginning of the kingdom," Weston said, seemingly aware of Gavinaugh's intense emotions.

Gavinaugh looked at Weston and relaxed slightly. Even as a Noble Knight he would have found the practice of slavery abominable, but only with the enlightenment of the Prince did he care about such things beyond the borders of Chessington. Now that Gavinaugh saw all people as equal in the eyes of the King, what was happening before him was appalling.

They rode near the auction and dismounted. Gavinaugh was amazed at how efficient the leadership of Santiok had become in this barbaric business. The main thoroughfare was crowded with people from all across the region. The traders and their slaves were cordoned off in a holding area, each waiting his turn for the auctioneer to sell the bounty of stolen human lives. The city's leadership received a fee and a commission for each sale as payment for organizing and hosting the trade. Their own guard force kept the whole affair orderly and also served to deny any other such trades from occurring within this region of the kingdom. Their monopoly was efficient and rewarded both the slave traders and the people who purchased slaves within the city. The fate of the slaves themselves varied greatly. Some became servants at large estates. The stronger men were often put to work on large farms or even at the walls of a castle lord. A few unfortunate ones were taken to a distant place where they reputedly served as entertainment in vicious tournaments to the death.

Gavinaugh struggled with being near such base treatment of people, but realized that only the compassion of the Prince could ultimately abolish such detestable practices.

A sale had just finished, and the auctioneer motioned to a guard to bring the next slave forward. A large man in shackles was taken to the front of the platform.

"Here is a fine specimen of brawn that is well suited to labor on any estate. Sir Boron, I hear you are in need of an extra hand. What a fine opportunity for you today! Or perhaps we have a buyer from Thecia looking for a swordsman to entertain his crowd. I tell you, this is one of the best to cross this platform in months. The bidding will start at fifty florins."

The response from the crowd was apparent, for this was an unusually high starting bid.

A wealthy man nodded, and the bidding began. After an exchange of bids between the wealthy man and another man with unfamiliar attire, the deal closed at 125 florins. The slave trader smiled broadly in anticipation of his profit.

Gavinaugh and Weston worked their way to the front of the crowd as the next slave was brought onto the auction platform. A young woman with long brown hair that was twisted and gnarled was pushed to the front of the platform. Though her head was lowered, she glanced briefly at the crowd, and Gavinaugh saw bitterness and hatred emanating from the depths of her soul. The shackles on her feet and wrists had worn the flesh beneath raw. The guard pushed her the last few paces, and she turned toward him as if to attack. The guard put his hand to his sword. She turned away and took a final step forward. Once at the front of the platform, she stared at the planks beneath her feet, her hair nearly covering her face. Her body was thin, and a tattered dress hung loosely from her frame.

The crowd began to chortle, and the auctioneer struggled to find the right words to begin.

"Settle down and let's get on with business. Who will open the bidding at twenty florins for this, ah…excellent worker?" he asked.

The crowd roared in laughter.

"Why is everyone laughing?" Gavinaugh asked a fat fellow he was standing next to. He had to ask twice since the man's own laughter was deafening. His double chin jiggled with each guttural expulsion.

"That's Crazy Keanna. They couldn't *pay* someone to take her!" He laughed all the harder.

The auctioneer tried to settle the crowd. "Ten florins is a steal… Who will start at ten?"

Gavinaugh questioned the man further. "Why not?"

"You're obviously not from these parts. Crazy Keanna has run away a hundred times, and she even stabbed her last owner." He pointed to a man standing near one of the slave traders. His arm was bandaged, and the anger on his face was evident.

"She's been sold a dozen times and beaten dozens more, but quite frankly no one dares buy her 'cause she's a vicious creature. I'm surprised she's survived this long." The auctioneer lowered the bid to five florins, and the fat man laughed even harder. So did the rest of the crowd.

Gavinaugh could stand it no longer. He broke from the crowd and walked into the open space before the waist-high platform. The crowd hushed somewhat.

"Are you making a bid, sir?" the auctioneer asked.

Gavinaugh looked up at the pathetic young woman, but her eyes were now blank and empty. He turned to face the people.

"People of Santiok, I am Sir Gavinaugh, from the city of Chessington. The King of Arrethtrae never intended for people to be bought and sold like cattle. What you are doing here is wrong!"

"Guards!" The auctioneer called, and four men brandishing swords came from each side of the platform. The tension escalated quickly, and the crowd began to murmur.

There was no hesitation in the approach of the guards. Weston stepped forward to intercept the two guards coming from the left and drew his sword. Gavinaugh did so as well, contending with the guards from the right.

"I was hoping for a little different response," he said to Weston over his shoulder.

Weston glanced back. "I can see that traveling with you is going to continue to be an adventure."

The guards immediately brought their swords to bear on them. Gavinaugh and Weston fought back to back as the guards spread their attack. The crowd backed away to allow room for fighting and twittered with excitement.

Swords flew swiftly to meet each slice and cut. The guards found themselves in a fight against two superbly trained swordsmen who did not falter. Gavinaugh met the slice of one guard with the flat of his blade, countered to put the man in retreat, then brought his sword powerfully across to his other opponent. With a quick thrust, he pierced the sword arm of his opponent just enough to cause him to withdraw. He then focused on his remaining opponent. He feigned a retreat, and the guard executed a thrust at Gavinaugh's chest. Gavinaugh parried and put a bind on the guard's sword that wrenched it from his grip. Gavinaugh made a quick thrust to put the man in retreat, which kept the man from recovering his sword.

He turned to help Weston, but one of his opponents was already backing away due to a wound in his thigh, and the other seemed hesitant to engage again. The auctioneer motioned across the street to a reserve of guards that began making their way through the crowd. Gavinaugh jumped onto the platform and held his sword high in the air.

"Citizens of Santiok…what gives you the right to consider yourselves more worthy than any of the slaves here? Is it your wealth? Is it your might? If I were to challenge any here to a duel and defeat him, would I not then be mightier than he? Does this give me the right to rule him as his owner? If so, then who here will challenge me?"

The crowd was silent, and the slave lifted her head to look at Gavinaugh. He glanced toward her and noticed that her blank stare was gone and her eyes were now angry and penetrating.

Gavinaugh turned to the auctioneer and pointed his sword at him. At that the guards halted their approach. "You—what gives you the right to sell people and not yourself be sold?" Gavinaugh felt the fire of the Prince flowing through his veins.

"There is none more mighty in all the land than the King, Himself, and yet He gives all people of Arrethtrae the right to choose their own course. I am a free man and yet choose to serve the King because He is good, just, and honorable above all. Listen and understand! When the kingdom turned away from the King, He sent His only Son to come to this wretched land and teach us of His great compassion. So great was His love that the Prince gave His life as a substitute for what we ourselves deserve. Now He lives and will come again to the land as our King. Open your eyes and accept the truth."

Gavinaugh sheathed his sword and walked to the young woman in shackles.

"Whether prince or pauper, nobleman or peasant, freeman or slave, the King sees all as equal and does not respect any because of wealth or position. He looks for true nobility in the hearts of men and women. For this reason I implore you to follow the ways of the King and His Son."

Gavinaugh lifted his arm toward the young woman named Keanna. "Free your slaves, and show compassion to your fellow citizens, as the King has shown His compassion to you."

Some in the crowd were moved by the emotional words Gavinaugh spoke, but many began to ridicule and taunt him. Throughout his oration Keanna's eyes never left him.

"You are as crazy as Crazy Keanna!" one man shouted.

"Go back to Chessington, and keep your foolish notions to yourself!" another shouted.

"Off the platform!"

The auctioneer stepped forward and held up his arms. "Perhaps this good man is right!"

The crowd quieted; many looked surprised.

"Although profitable, this is a detestable business we are in." He motioned for the guard with the keys to approach.

Gavinaugh sensed the sarcasm and saw twenty to thirty guards gathering nearby.

"To show good faith in our intentions to honor the King and this man's eloquent speech, we shall begin releasing our slaves right now."

The guard began unlocking the woman's shackles. She was still staring fiercely at Gavinaugh.

"By the King's authority I release this slave to your care!" he exclaimed as the last binding fell from Keanna. She did not move.

The crowd laughed and resumed their heckling. Gavinaugh was

not angry but felt pity for the woman, for the people, for the whole land. They did not understand that the consequence of their folly would be great. He walked and stood before Keanna.

"You are free to go," he said gently.

Keanna looked into his eyes with an anger that Gavinaugh did not understand. She lifted her hands and looked at the raw rings about her wrists. Then she reached back and slapped Gavinaugh across the face with all her might. The crowd erupted in laughter as Keanna jumped from the platform and frantically pushed her way through the crowd. Once clear, she ran down the open street.

By now a full contingent of guards had surrounded the platform.

"Leave at once or you will die!" the auctioneer commanded.

Gavinaugh jumped from the platform. He and Weston exited peacefully and retreated to their horses.

"They are all fools!" Weston said.

"Not all," came a voice from behind them.

Gavinaugh and Weston turned to see that four men had followed them from the crowd.

"We heard your words and know that there is truth in what you say. We want to hear more," one of the men said, and the others nodded their agreement.

"I am Gavinaugh. This is Weston."

"I am Turner. This is Aldrich, Denley, and Reed," the man said as he pointed to each of his friends.

"We will gladly tell you all, gentlemen. Is there a place we can talk?" Gavinaugh asked.

"Yes. Just up the street on the left I have a shop," Turner said.

Gavinaugh nodded. "Very well. We shall meet you there shortly. I need to find the lass that took flight and try to help her."

"We will assist you, but our chances are slim. She is as slippery as a fish," Reed said.

"Where might she go?"

"Perhaps to steal food…perhaps to the country. It would be wise if we split up and met back at my shop before dusk. It's just over there," the man said and pointed to his shop.

"Very well."

Gavinaugh and Weston mounted their horses and galloped in the direction they last saw her run and then split up at the next thorough-fare. Gavinaugh was confused by the girl's reaction toward him and wondered if looking for her was really such a good idea. He rode by a bread shop and saw the owner swearing and looking up the street.

"Has a young woman been by?" he asked.

"You mean the wench who stole my bread?"

Gavinaugh reached into his pocket for money to pay for the bread. "Which way did she go?"

The man indicated up the street, and Gavinaugh rode in that direction. He slowed his horse to a walk.

"Can you help me, Triumph?" he said. The animal snorted.

A little farther up, Triumph stopped between a candle maker's shop and an inn. Gavinaugh dismounted and slowly walked between the wooden and stone structures to the alleyway behind. He could hear two pigs foraging in a nearby heap. Just behind the inn, he saw Keanna ravenously eating the bread. She was hunkered down on the ground with her back to him.

"Would you like some water with that?" he asked.

Keanna startled. She jumped up and began to look for a way to escape.

"Please don't run… I want to help you." He offered his water flask to her.

Once again she stared hard at him. She cautiously took the flask and drank heavily, never taking her eyes off Gavinaugh. She ate and drank some more.

"Where are you from, Keanna?" he asked.

"Not from this wretched place," she said between bites.

Gavinaugh could not help feeling great compassion for her. She looked as though she was slightly younger than he. Although she apparently was capable of violent action, he wondered what her story was and how she had come to such a sorry state.

"Where will you go now?" he asked.

She looked at him somewhat perplexed. "Away…away from here…away from everyone!"

"What will you do?"

"Why do you care?" she asked angrily.

Gavinaugh looked at her gnarled, matted hair and dirty, bruised face. Her upper lip was swollen and cracked. Dried blood filled the crevice made by a recent strike. "Because I have learned from the Prince that every soul in the kingdom needs compassion…even a slave girl who hates the world."

Keanna stopped chewing, and for one brief moment Gavinaugh saw the harsh lines of anger on her face recede.

"Let me help you. There is an inn right here where I will be staying. I will arrange for a bath, clothes, and food for you. If you choose to leave, I won't stand in your way."

Keanna's eyes narrowed as if to question Gavinaugh's sincerity. Something connected in her thoughts, and she slowly nodded her head in agreement. He waited for her to finish the bread and then took her to the front of the inn. As they passed by Triumph, he nickered and went to Keanna. She stopped and stroked his neck. The horse nudged her affectionately.

"I think he likes you," Gavinaugh said.

Keanna didn't reply. She leaned on the horse and rested her head against his muscular neck. Triumph responded gently and allowed her to take comfort from him.

In the inn, Gavinaugh made arrangements with the innkeeper and his wife. They seemed fair and kind, although they were somewhat cautious regarding Keanna.

"Once she is fed and clean, give her a room with a soft bed to sleep in. Here is payment through tonight," he said. They accepted his money, and he left to find Weston and the other men.

Back at Turner's shop, the four men listened anxiously to Gavinaugh as he told them of the story of the Prince. There was a yearning in their hearts that was evident by the sparkle in their eyes. In this dark corner of the kingdom, Gavinaugh and Weston found men of hope and courage who longed for the truth that would transcend the despairing pit of commonality. He told them of the past and of the future and also of the silent raging battle between the forces of the Prince and of Lucius.

"What you tell us is glorious to hear. What must we do?" Reed asked.

"Simply believe, tell others, and prepare. You must train for battle against the Dark Knight and his Shadow Warriors," Gavinaugh replied.

"But we know nothing of warfare," Turner said.

"We will train you to become Knights of the Prince. In our absence you must continue what we have taught you and increase in your knowledge and skill with the sword," Gavinaugh said. "Such a choice may cost you everything, but the freedom and joy you will gain in your service to the King and the Prince will be more precious than gold. Are you willing?"

"We are," they replied in unison.

Gavinaugh knighted the four men, and the haven at Santiok was begun.

By the day's end, the passion of these four men to learn the art of the sword and to live by the Code was invigorating. They determined to meet each day to continue training.

"What of the slave girl?" Aldrich asked Gavinaugh.

"She is at the inn. I arranged for food, clothing, and a room to sleep in tonight," he said.

"I'd be surprised if she is still there in the morning."

"Why do you say that?" Gavinaugh asked.

"Because from what I have heard, she has tried to either run away from or injure every master she's ever had," Aldrich replied.

"I am not her master, and she is free to leave at any time," Gavinaugh said.

Weston and Gavinaugh returned to the inn for the evening meal. Gavinaugh knocked on Keanna's door, but there was no response. "Our supper is prepared if you would like to eat." He spoke to the closed door, not sure if she was even in the room.

In the dining room, Weston and Gavinaugh were seated when Keanna descended the stairs to join them. Although her countenance was still as hard as stone, something spectacular glimmered beneath the fury of her eyes, and Gavinaugh was momentarily distracted. Her dark brown hair, now clean and combed, hung loosely about her shoulders, contrasting with her captivating, sky blue eyes. Her face was clean, but the bruises of her prior torment were still evident. Keanna ate her meal in silence, as Gavinaugh and Weston discussed the training and future plans for the newly founded haven.

The next morning, Keanna joined them again for breakfast.

"Did you sleep well, Keanna?" Weston asked.

She looked at him and nodded.

"We will be training today, but one of the men has offered his home to us to stay in. We can take you there now if you'd like," Gavinaugh said to Keanna.

She stared at him blankly, and Gavinaugh wondered if perhaps she hadn't understood him.

"I will go with you," she finally replied.

Gavinaugh looked at Weston, and he nodded his approval.

They trained the new Knights of the Prince for many days, and many men and women joined their ranks daily. The haven of Santiok became strong in the ways of the Code and of the Prince. Although Keanna was always with them, and in particular with Gavinaugh, she did not warm to them in the least. She took it upon herself to care for their horses, and the only time Gavinaugh saw her soften was when she groomed Triumph. On one occasion, Gavinaugh caught Keanna staring at him with a countenance full of malice. She quickly diverted her eyes, which left Gavinaugh wondering. Later he made an attempt to talk to her, but a wall of bitterness surrounded her like an impenetrable fortress. He was confused as to why she chose to be with him throughout the day when she despised him so. He finally attributed it to the harsh life she had lived and was hopeful that over time she would come to accept the compassion of the Prince.

One day during a break in the training, Gavinaugh went to Triumph and found Keanna patting and talking softly to the horse. She did not notice him, and in that moment Gavinaugh saw Keanna in a way that opened his eyes to the beautiful creature she once was. The bruises and swelling had vanished, and for a moment there was a look of peace on her face. Although his intent was not to spy on her, he was oddly mesmerized by this rare moment of tenderness and by her true beauty. She happened to glance in his direction, and like the splash of a rock in a perfectly still pool of water, the reflection of beauty was gone in an instant. She scowled and was visibly angry at his observation of her. Triumph nickered and seemed to try and soothe her, but she stiffened and turned her back to Gavinaugh.

He walked over to Triumph. "I need to retrieve an item from my pack," he said, slightly embarrassed.

She left him and returned to the training area. From that moment on, Keanna seemed to avoid Gavinaugh and even stopped coming to the training of the knights—but she did not leave them.

Upon their return to Turner's home a few weeks later, Gavinaugh and Weston discussed their next course of action.

"These men are ready to be on their own," Gavinaugh said.

"Yes, I agree," Weston replied. "The heart of the Prince is strong within them."

"We must return here again to encourage them, but there are others who need to hear of the Prince."

"Where to now?"

Gavinaugh smiled at his friend. "You have been away from your family for many weeks, my friend. I plan to travel north to Penwell, but you should return to your family."

"I do miss them terribly. Cresthaven is not far off the road to Penwell. Will you come and have a meal with us at least? The children would love to see you again," Weston said.

Gavinaugh smiled as he thought of the tender little faces of Addy and Keaton. He nodded his approval.

The following morning, Gavinaugh, Weston, and Keanna left Santiok for Cresthaven. Toward evening, they set up camp at the base of a small waterfall near the edge of the woods. They were tired from the day's journey. The stillness of the night and the soothing sound of the waterfall welcomed them to rest. After building a fire and eating some of their provisions, Gavinaugh and Weston retired to their bedrolls, but Keanna did not seem to yield to her weariness. Weston fell asleep at once, and as Gavinaugh drowsed, the edge of his mind felt a vague surprise at seeing Keanna sitting by the fire, seemingly waiting for something. But then sleep overtook him.

CHAPTER FIVE

THE
EXECUTIONER

 Keanna waited long into the night, all the while calling the memories of her anguished past to the forefront of her mind, for the fire of vengeance burned hot within her heart. The bitterness she harbored in her marrow had changed her over time into the angry young woman she was today. For years, she had only dreamed of vengeance—until a few weeks ago, when she saw Gavinaugh at the slave auction in Santiok.

Keanna quietly rose from her bed. The slight rustling of the leaves and grass beneath her feet was lost in the gentle sound of the waterfall nearby. The turmoil in her soul rose bitterly as she remembered the heartless murder of her parents and the cries of terror from her younger siblings. She considered the light of the full moon a gift, for she wanted to see the face of the one who had brought such pain to her life.

Gavinaugh was lying on his back with a blanket covering his body. It seemed too perfect—his sword and long-knife were right beside him. Keanna went to him, knelt down, and grasped the long-knife. The handle felt good in her hand, and the fury in her heart was satisfying. She looked at the face of Gavinaugh and married his image with the image of her murdered parents. She lifted the knife high above her head, poised for the strike that would appease her desire for vengeance.

She searched for the perfect target, watching his chest rise and fall with each breath. He had pierced her heart with sorrow, and now she would pierce his with his own blade. She tightened all of her muscles. Gavinaugh stirred, and she froze. His hand moved beneath the blanket, and he scratched his neck. The hand returned to his side, pulling the blanket off his chest, and he was still once again.

Keanna slowly released her breath. In that moment, the reality of taking the life of another stunned her, and she hesitated. She had wounded other masters before, but always in self-defense. This was different. She steeled herself against inner petitions of mercy and readied her blade once again. There was his heart, but the light of the full moon now revealed something she had not seen earlier. With the blanket off his chest, the emblem of the Prince was now as clear as a banner atop a castle wall. Her blade would have to first pierce the mark of the Prince before penetrating the heart of her nemesis. Gavinaugh's words of the Prince seemed to resonate in her mind, and she could not make them go away...words of love, compassion, and mercy. She hated the words and yet was drawn to them.

Her grip on vengeance loosened and she wavered. Her muscles began to ache, as did her heart. She looked up to the stars to forget the image on Gavinaugh's chest, but it was engraved in her mind as a backdrop to the strange story of a man who seemed to change the hearts of others. She fought against the possibility that this man's heart had truly changed. Her eyes filled with tears as the war within her soul culminated. In a final charge of defiance, she plunged the knife downward toward her victim.

Keanna rose up and ran into the woods, not waiting to see the outcome of her action. She fled the pain—the memories—and now she fled the Prince. She ran, but there was no place to hide. Tears of torment rose up like a flood, and she could not control the deep sobbing that swelled within her bosom. She ran until she was swallowed up by the trees in the woods. The yellow light of the moon fell upon a large, jagged rock in a small clearing, and she collapsed beside it. She wondered at the purpose of such a cruel life and wished her existence would end.

"Gavinaugh!" Weston exclaimed. The hilt of the long-knife stood straight, proclaiming the actions of the executioner.

Gavinaugh blinked and wiped away the fog of sleep.

"What is it?" he asked groggily.

Weston pointed, and Gavinaugh turned to see his long-knife plunged deep into the earth beside his chest. The rush within his muscles snapped him into full consciousness in an instant. He reached for his sword and searched for the enemy.

"Who?" he asked. He was grateful that his life was still his own.

"I don't know, but Keanna is missing!"

Gavinaugh quickly rose up and felt fear rise in his heart. "No!" he exclaimed. "Why would they take her and not kill us?"

Weston shook his head. "I don't know. They can't be far, though, for her bed is still warm."

Gavinaugh became fierce. He had felt responsible for Keanna ever since meeting her weeks earlier at the slave auction. Though she had shown no tenderness at all toward him, he could not deny that his sense of obligation as her protector was transcended at times by something deeper. He fastened his sword.

"We *must* find her!" he exclaimed.

"Yes, but where do we look, and how many will we face?" Weston said.

They searched the ground surrounding their camp and found no sign of a struggle. Gavinaugh was thankful for the light of the moon, but searching at night proved difficult.

"There are no tracks in the bank of the stream," Gavinaugh said. "You search downstream and I'll search up."

Weston nodded. The men separated, and Gavinaugh desperately

searched for a sign that would indicate the direction taken by Keanna's captors. He followed the stream for a bit and then patterned his search until he found a spot where the tree branches were pushed slightly apart. He knelt beside a single set of footprints in the green moss of the forest floor. The direction was clear, but Gavinaugh was very confused. *There are no other footprints… Did she flee from her captors?* He looked down at his knife, and an inconceivable thought began to enter his mind.

It was quiet here, away from the stream and the waterfall. Gavinaugh stared back at the footprints and placed his hand within the indentation.

"Where are you, Keanna?" he whispered to himself, still not certain if there were enemies nearby.

Gavinaugh heard the faint sounds of weeping filtering through the woods, and he recognized the delicate voice of Keanna. He rose up and quickened his pace to find her. He drew his sword as he came closer. Her sobbing was deep, and his apprehension grew. He searched the surroundings in all directions as he approached, but there were no enemies.

He came to her in a clearing, where she was doubled over beside a large, jagged rock. He knelt on one knee beside her and placed a gentle hand on her shoulder. Keanna screamed and recoiled from his touch. She backed into the rock behind her.

"Don't touch me!" she shouted between sobs. Tears streamed down her face.

He looked at her, bewildered. She stared back, and Gavinaugh saw the torment of her heart in her face.

"What happened… Are you hurt?" he asked tenderly.

"Why did you leave me…why?" she asked.

Gavinaugh was even further confused. "What do you mean? I have been near you since we met."

"No! You left me to those animals that killed my parents. You could have saved all of us, but you turned away…you left me to those…those…murderers! I hate you!" Keanna buried her face in her hands and wept even harder.

As lightning explodes across the sky, an image of a mud-covered, terrified girl running toward him on the road to Cartelbrook long ago before flashed across his mind's eye. His heart sank in painful remorse as he realized that Keanna was that girl. Only now did he understand that he had abandoned her to the brutish Shadow Warriors because she was an Outdweller. He lowered his head and felt ashamed as he once again faced the pain of his former life as a Noble Knight.

"Keanna…I…I…," he struggled for words, but everything seemed wholly inadequate.

For a moment nothing was said. Her weeping eventually diminished.

"I tried to kill you," she said quietly.

"I don't blame you. What stopped you?"

She looked away. "I saw the emblem of the Prince on your tunic. I don't know why, but I couldn't once I saw it."

"I am a different man, Keanna. This same Prince has changed me. If I could right all of my wrongs, I would a thousand times over. I am so very sorry I ever hurt you." Tears filled his eyes—he was cut to the core as he realized how that single act of abandonment had destroyed a family and the heart of the young woman before him.

She looked at him and did not answer, but the fierce anger in her eyes seemed absent.

"Your words of the Prince keep filling my mind, and I have not been able to make them go away," she said.

He turned and leaned against the rock beside her.

"That is why I couldn't be around you any longer in Santiok," she said. "Every time I heard you speak to the people about the Prince, I felt my grip on revenge loosen. I wanted you to pay for the pain you put me and my family through." Keanna began to weep softly again.

Gavinaugh lowered his head. "I have caused many people much pain, Keanna, and I deserve death more than any other. But I swear to you this day that my purpose is now to bring healing by the power of the Prince. He has granted me the undeserved forgiveness that I longed for. I can hardly ask such a thing from you, even though it is my heart's desire. My hope is that perhaps one day you will not hate me quite as much as I deserve."

Keanna was silent, and Gavinaugh expected nothing else. His heart had been stirred earlier by her presence in his life, and now he felt an overwhelming compassion and responsibility for her as never before.

After a lengthy time of silence, Gavinaugh stood and offered his hand to Keanna.

"Sir Weston is also searching for you and I fear is very concerned. I can't leave you here. Please come with me," he said tenderly.

She did not recoil as before, but took his hand and stood. They walked back to camp and rejoined Weston. Few words were exchanged as they tried to regain what was left of the night in sleep, but Gavinaugh could not rest. It was his turn to look upon the sleeping form of another. For the first time since Santiok, he thought she looked at peace. He remained watchful the rest of the night, not daring to falter in protecting his charge.

CHAPTER SIX

HEALING THE FAIR OF HEART

Penwell lay far north of the Forest of Renault. Gavinaugh's intent was to take the story of the Prince to many cities and villages along the way, establish havens, and make Knights of the Prince of all who were willing to follow. However, Gavinaugh could not deny that he was looking forward to an interlude at Cresthaven. During their journey, Keanna did not seem spiteful toward him any longer, but she was certainly distant.

The reunion with Marie, Addy, and Keaton was a delight, and they implored Gavinaugh to stay a couple of days with them before traveling on to Penwell. He acquiesced, in no small part due to the pleading of Addy and Keaton. Gavinaugh's heart was particularly warmed by the change he saw in Keanna. Over those two days, the joyful spirits of the children and the tender affection that Marie bestowed on her seemed to heal many wounds in Keanna's soul. This led Gavinaugh to linger a few more days. Before long, Addy and Keaton had captured the affection of Keanna's heart, and Gavinaugh noticed that she quickly became as a big sister to the children.

Occasionally there were moments when Keanna became intensely sad, and Gavinaugh believed it was because Weston's family reminded her of her own. One evening during supper, a humorous story about

Addy was told that brought laughter to all. Keanna witnessed the joy of the family and seemed to be overcome with sadness. She lowered her head, and the others grew silent.

"What's wrong, Keanna?" Addy asked as she gently touched her arm. At their request, she and Keaton had been seated on each side of Keanna.

Keanna looked at her and tried to smile, but a tear fell from her cheek. Keaton rose from his chair and put his arms around Keanna's neck. She leaned into his little body and seemed to melt in the warmth of his loving heart. He remained in her embrace until the grief of her past had fallen away. Addy rested her head on Keanna's shoulder, and Gavinaugh saw the love of the Prince in the children's tenderness.

Of such is His kingdom, he thought. Gavinaugh was greatly moved by Addy and Keaton's simple acts of compassion. The moment lingered until Keanna relaxed her hug. Keaton looked at her as if to say, *Will you be all right now?*

Keanna smiled and wiped away her tears. She seemed embarrassed.

"Papa says that when you're sad, it's best to do something that will make you happy," Addy said. She furrowed her brow as if she were thinking hard. A big smile crossed her lips, and she looked directly at Keanna. "Playing hide-and-seek always makes me happy. Do you want to play hide-and-seek with us?"

Keanna laughed. "I'd love to." She seemed relieved to have a reason to leave the table. Before long, laughter and giggles filled the house, and Gavinaugh marveled at the unfolding beauty of the woman who just weeks earlier had been an embittered, battered slave girl. Like a rosebush breaking free from the grasp of winter, the warmth in her smile drew the children to her. She was slender and slightly shorter than most young women, but Keanna's poise and humble spirit conveyed a noble beauty that her prior persecution had not been able to erase. Gavinaugh could hardly stop watching her, mesmerized by the transformation and the clarity of her true, tender heart. He had never seen her smile, let alone laugh...until now.

"She seems like quite a young woman, Gavinaugh," Marie said with a smile. Gavinaugh, Weston, and Marie were sitting at the dining room table catching glimpses of the playful antics of the children and Keanna through the arched doorway.

"She has been through a great deal," he replied. "The children are so good for her, and your kindness toward her is truly a blessing, Marie. Thank you."

At one point Keanna grabbed unsuspecting Keaton from his hiding place beneath the grand staircase and tickled him. He giggled and struggled free, leaving Keanna smiling. She happened to glance into the dining room, and Gavinaugh's eyes caught hers, but her smile did not diminish as he would have expected. He was not certain if she was truly looking at him, but in that moment Gavinaugh was taken and his heart was inclined toward her, for the radiance of her smile illuminated his soul as never before. The exchange was brief, but the impression was permanent.

Until now Gavinaugh had considered his role with regard to her as protector and provider only, but something changed in that single glance, and now his heart was no longer his own. He could not explain the strange feeling in the pit of his stomach, nor did he understand it—it was something new and powerful. He tried to reason out the foolishness of what he thought must be a new affection for her, but logic found no place to wrest the anchor of love from his heart. He was certain, however, that she had no such feelings toward him because of the pain he had brought into her life. All he could really hope for was forgiveness.

"...do you think, Gavinaugh?" Weston asked, apparently finishing a question that Gavinaugh hadn't heard.

Gavinaugh jerked his head around. "I'm sorry... Ah, what do I think about what?" He was embarrassed by his distraction.

What was that? Never before had his attention been so diverted.

Weston glanced toward Marie with a perplexed look, but Marie just smiled.

"I said that maybe it would be wise to have Keanna stay here with us for a time. She seems to be doing so well, and the children absolutely love her," Weston said.

"Yes, that is an excellent idea," Gavinaugh said, attempting a thoughtful pose. "Where I am going will potentially be dangerous. It would be best for her."

When they offered Keanna the opportunity to stay, she accepted, and Gavinaugh found himself strangely disappointed, but he knew it was for the best.

The following morning, Gavinaugh prepared to leave. Keanna held Triumph's reins and stroked his neck as Gavinaugh embraced Weston and his family. He then turned and looked upon Keanna.

"I am pleased that you are here with Weston and Marie. They will take good care of you," he said.

"Yes…I am grateful." She looked briefly into Gavinaugh's eyes.

"Farewell then, Keanna," he said and bowed his head slightly.

"Farewell, Gavinaugh."

It was the first time she had spoken his name, and as he rode away, he could not help replaying their parting in his mind many times.

How ridiculous! he thought. *I have a mission to fulfill and no time for such silliness.*

He set his course toward Penwell, but the memory of her voice speaking his name accompanied him for many miles.

Gavinaugh journeyed through various towns and villages, carrying the story of the Prince to all who would listen. There was no mediocre welcome at any of the towns—he was either received heartily or rejected most fiercely. It seemed to Gavinaugh that the Prince created great division among all people.

Having finally arrived in Penwell, he discovered that the people there were most irritated by his words and his presence. He had managed to recruit a dozen men as Knights of the Prince, but the leadership of the city was quickly becoming hostile toward him. In spite of this,

Gavinaugh found one young recruit who inspired him, for he was zealous for the Code and the Prince. Sandon at first seemed quiet, not because of shyness, but because his words were well thought out before he spoke them. On serious matters, he preferred to listen first and then speak. Gavinaugh also discovered a keen sense of humor in the young man, which often surprised those who did not know him well. Sandon's hair was dark and his jaw was strong. Gavinaugh sensed his loyalty to the Prince and to him.

The regional governor had issued numerous edicts ordering Gavinaugh to cease his activities and leave the region, but Gavinaugh continued. One day, Sandon stood beside him on the main thoroughfare and boldly petitioned the people to listen to the words of the Prince. When a crowd had gathered, Gavinaugh once again shared the story of the Prince and His life-changing message. What he didn't realize was that a force of guards was gathering nearby to end what Governor Thurman saw as a threat to his power and to their way of life. Within moments, they were surrounded by an overwhelming force and bound in fetters.

Gavinaugh and Sandon were briskly taken to the office of the magistrate, where the governor looked on, and the trial and sentencing was conducted in less time than it took to eat an apple. Sandon was sentenced to six months in the dungeons, but Gavinaugh was to be beaten and cast outside the city limits. The sentence of beating was really a sentence of death, since the thugs executing the sentence often would not stop until there was no sign of life in their victim.

"Do not lose heart, Sandon," Gavinaugh called to his companion as they were separated.

"Nor you, Sir Gavinaugh," Sandon called back, but there was sadness in his voice.

Four burly men took Gavinaugh to a rock quarry beyond the surrounding hills of the city. His bonds were not loosed, so his unprotected body bore the full blow of each fist and foot. When he could no longer stand, he fell to his knees and the rocks beneath him turned red with his blood. The pain of the beating began to fade until it seemed his body was completely numb. He fell facedown with nothing to soften the impact and could vaguely feel the jarring of his body across the jagged rocks beneath him as the beating continued, but the pain was nearly gone. A dark cloud descended from the sky and enveloped his mind, giving him a final escape from the brutality of the thugs.

"There are so many people, my Lord…so many," Gavinaugh said as he walked beside the majestic Prince along the shore of a beautiful sea that shined like clear crystal.

"Do not be discouraged, my friend. For every one you reach, My words are multiplied a hundredfold and will not return empty. Rise up and carry on." The Prince stopped and placed a hand on Gavinaugh's shoulder. He smiled a gentle smile, and Gavinaugh felt the warmth of the Prince's glory empower his soul. His words felt like sweet water to his lips.

"I will, my Prince. With all of my strength, I will!"

The Prince left him, and Gavinaugh began to feel very tired.

"What do we do now?" a voice asked.

"There are other Followers in nearby villages. I think we should find them. Even though Gavinaugh is dead, the words of the Prince are not," another voice responded.

Gavinaugh felt a hand on his forehead, and with that touch, the pain from his entire body crashed upon his consciousness.

"He brought us such hope. Dare we go on without him?"

Gavinaugh now recognized this voice. It belonged to Fredrick.

Gavinaugh opened his eyes and heard the exclamations of his fellow knights as they gasped in shock. He slowly pulled himself to a standing position.

"Of course, we go on," Gavinaugh said and tried to smile through his swollen face. "The Prince expects no less."

The four men surrounding him looked as though they had seen a ghost and even backed away from him slightly.

"You were dead, Gavinaugh. I felt your chest and there was nothing. How…how can this be?" Fredrick said in disbelief.

Gavinaugh felt as though he might faint, but Jonnas reached out and supported him. They leaned him against a large stone nearby.

"To live for the Prince brings hope to the kingdom." Gavinaugh labored to catch his breath. "If I should die in that service, my end will be in honor. Either way I gain. My life is in the hands of the Prince, not the brutes of Penwell."

The men were still amazed as they searched for a cloth from their packs to wipe the blood from his wounds.

"What I don't understand is why they left this water flask when I am certain they also thought you were dead," Jonnas said as he handed the flask to Gavinaugh.

He took a drink from the flask, and the water was sweet, like the words of the Prince. He felt the cool sensation in his stomach. Although his body ached, the healing had begun. He looked across the rock quarry and into the vast kingdom beyond. The words of the Prince would bring healing to a land in pain, and the forces of the Dark Knight would one day be crushed by the heel of the Prince. Of that he was certain!

CHAPTER SEVEN

THE DUNGEONS OF PENWELL

After a few days of healing, Gavinaugh resumed his training with the Knights of the Prince in Penwell. He also continued to recruit, and their numbers grew steadily. Under the most severe persecution, Gavinaugh had found the strongest devotion to the Prince. Those who chose to join them did so with full knowledge of the possibility of hardship, so none came halfheartedly.

As the haven of Penwell grew, so did the regional governor's anger. Eventually Gavinaugh was again arrested and thrown into the dungeon.

"You are alive!" Sandon exclaimed. Gavinaugh had been cast into the cell across the aisle. Sandon stood at his cell door and smiled broadly.

"Sandon, it is good to see you!" Gavinaugh said.

"Quiet!" barked the guard as he turned and left.

"Don't mind him," Sandon said. "He's just having a bad day. I made Followers of the last two guards, so now they won't let me talk to them anymore."

Gavinaugh laughed. "Somehow I'm not surprised, my friend."

The two men rejoiced at their reunion and encouraged each other greatly.

Three days later, the guards brought a third captive into the dungeon and cast him into the cell next to Sandon.

"Weston? What in the kingdom are you doing here?" Gavinaugh asked.

"Well, I heard there was trouble in Penwell, and it didn't take me long to figure out that you were in the middle of it, so I came to see if I could help," Weston said.

"I see that you are doing a fine job of helping," Gavinaugh said. "Sir Weston of Cresthaven, meet Sir Sandon of Penwell."

The two men shook hands through the bars of their cells.

"The governor here was not very tolerant of me once he discovered I was associated with you," Weston said. "At least he released Keanna, though."

"Keanna? You brought Keanna here?" Gavinaugh asked.

Weston nodded. "When word came to us that you were in trouble, she insisted on coming with me and would not have it any other way."

Gavinaugh was not happy that she was in a city that was so hostile toward the Followers.

"I thought that perhaps since she found it no longer necessary to kill me, she wouldn't care to ever be near me again," Gavinaugh said.

"You know, Gavinaugh, you seem to have that effect on a lot of people," Sandon said with a grin. "Now you have a woman who wants to kill you as well?"

"Yes, what is it about you?" Weston joined in.

"That would be quite humorous, gentlemen, if it weren't for the fact that tomorrow we may *all* be sentenced to death."

It was a sobering thought, for they knew that the governor was extremely concerned about their influence in the city.

Two more days passed, and their only connection with the outside world was the guard and a small barred window at the far end of the aisle. By day it gave enough light to see the rotten food they were fed, but at night the dungeon cells became black with darkness.

One evening, the darkness came early to their cells as they heard a storm building outside. The occasional crash of thunder echoed down to them through the corridor. The door to the dungeon opened, and a guard entered with an oil lamp. Behind him followed Governor Thurman. The governor was pompous and carried himself with an air of arrogance. He stopped before Gavinaugh's cell.

"You are a persistent fellow, aren't you?" he said with a sneer.

Gavinaugh stood and walked to the cell door.

"I like to consider myself a peaceful ruler in this province, and you have brought great unrest to my people." The governor spoke with a condescending tone. He took the keys from the guard. "I could easily have you sentenced to death, but my reputation has already been tarnished by your apparent inability to die. And unfortunately, the people seem taken with you."

He took a step closer to Gavinaugh. "Why don't we make a deal? How about I have you all whipped and released, and you promise to never come back to my city again?" He dangled the keys in front of Gavinaugh as if to tease him.

Just then a current of air flowed through the dungeon. The guard's oil lamp flickered and went out, leaving them in total darkness. The governor muttered a curse beneath his breath.

"Don't just stand there. Get another lamp!" he shouted to the guard. Gavinaugh could hear the guard stumbling down the aisle and up the stairs to the guard room.

A powerful lightning bolt flashed, and its light was bright enough to momentarily illuminate the cells. What they saw in that instant shocked them all. Two massive warriors stood one pace away from the governor with their swords drawn and a visage of fierceness. The governor choked on his own exclamation and fell to his knees in terror.

"Release them!"

The voice was deep, and the sound of it shook one's bones. Gavinaugh could hear the governor's whimpering in the dark.

A moment later, the guard hurried back to the cells. As his light invaded the darkness, Gavinaugh could not see the warriors anywhere.

"What is wrong, Governor?" the guard asked, alarmed at what he saw.

The governor was cowering on the floor, and his face was white with fear. The guard helped him stand, but his knees could barely hold him up. He fumbled with the keys and finally found the one that opened Gavinaugh's cell. His hands were shaking so violently that he could not place the key in the keyhole. He finally gave them to the guard.

"Release them," he whispered.

"What?" the guard asked.

The governor looked at him and then shouted. *"Release them!"* He looked around as though a monster were coming to devour him.

The guard moved with great urgency and opened the cell doors. Gavinaugh, Weston, and Sandon exited their cells.

Gavinaugh approached the governor, who looked as though he might run.

"This isn't about you keeping your power intact in the region, Governor. It's about the King destroying the powers of darkness in the kingdom." Gavinaugh turned, and the three men left the dungeon.

They went to the haven, and there was great rejoicing among the knights. Keanna looked relieved to see them, and Gavinaugh was pleased to see her.

In the days that followed, the persecution of the Knights of the Prince all but stopped, and they were free to recruit, build, and train without threat of imprisonment. The haven quickly became a strong force in the region in spite of the challenges that had hindered its beginning.

Gavinaugh looked for opportunities to spend time with Keanna. He was careful to temper his actions despite his growing fondness for her, for there were times when he feared she still held him in contempt. At other times, she responded kindly but always remained quite reserved.

One evening, Gavinaugh went to check on Triumph and found

Keanna caring for him. There was a connection between her and the animal that he did not fully understand, but he didn't mind.

"How's Triumph tonight?" he said as he approached and stood on the opposite side of the horse.

"He is a magnificent horse. I've never seen another like him. Where did you get him?" she asked.

"He was a gift from a stranger my mother showed kindness to."

Triumph nickered as Gavinaugh stroked his neck. "He seems quite taken with you." He smiled at her.

Keanna stopped her grooming and came to the other side of Triumph's neck. She looked at Gavinaugh across Triumph's nose. Her eyes gleamed in the evening night, and Gavinaugh drew strength from her gaze.

"I have always been able to connect to some degree with the horses I've cared for, but Triumph is different." Her eyes diverted to the steed.

"It's almost as if he chose to connect with me first. I can almost sense his thoughts…and I suppose he can mine," she said. Then she looked away, as if she wished she hadn't said it.

"Is that so?" Gavinaugh said, resisting the temptation to tease her. "What does he think of me?"

She looked at him as if she were trying to decide if he was sincere. "He thinks you are quite headstrong and a bit too impulsive at times."

Gavinaugh smiled. "Well, in your next conversation with him, tell him that I'll try to work on that."

As if on cue, Triumph snorted.

"Oh, and he says that you don't feed him enough sweet apples," she said without cracking a smile. Now it was Gavinaugh's turn to try to discern if she was sincere. But then she grinned slightly, and he laughed at himself. Gavinaugh looked into her eyes, and she paused at his gaze before turning aside.

"I should be getting back," she said quickly and took a couple of steps toward the haven.

"Keanna."

She turned and looked at him. He wanted so much more than to exchange just a few words with her.

"I…I just wanted to thank you for taking such good care of Triumph," he said, looking for some sign from her that they might eventually become friends…and maybe more.

"You're welcome," she said and proceeded on her way.

Gavinaugh watched her disappear into the haven and then lingered with Triumph a bit longer.

"Well, Triumph, what do *you* say she thinks of me?" he asked.

The animal snorted and jerked his head from side to side.

"Yes, I suppose you're right."

"Talking to horses, are we?" came a voice from the darkness behind him.

Gavinaugh was startled—only a Silent Warrior could come upon him so stealthily. The owner of the voice stepped out from the shadows of the trees.

"Porunth!" Gavinaugh exclaimed. "It is good to see you!"

The two embraced. "And you, my friend."

They talked briefly, and then Porunth became quite serious.

"I am on a mission and have a message for you. You are to travel to Thecia and take the word of the Prince to that city. You must be vigilant, Gavinaugh, for we have received information that the forces of the Dark Knight are plotting to kill you. It is difficult to predict more than that, so you must be on guard at all times."

Gavinaugh looked at Porunth and nodded.

"I understand. Thank you," he said.

Porunth looked as if he needed to say something more, so Gavinaugh waited.

"This Keanna you have discovered…" Porunth paused and looked intently at his friend. Gavinaugh began to suspect that words of distress were soon to be spoken.

"She is apparently important to the kingdom in some fashion, for the Prince has commanded that you are to continue protecting and training her."

Gavinaugh was relieved and pleased.

Porunth put his hand on Gavinaugh's shoulder. "You must help heal her sorrow, for there is more to come," he said.

Gavinaugh wanted to ask more, but Porunth ended the conversation and prepared to leave. They exchanged farewells and parted.

Gavinaugh found it difficult to sleep that night. His mind flitted between thoughts of Keanna, Thecia, and the Dark Knight. Only when he focused on thoughts of the Prince did he find the peace and elusive rest his body sought.

The next morning, Weston looked at Gavinaugh and seemed to know what was ahead.

"Where to?" he asked.

Gavinaugh was a bit surprised by Weston's discernment.

"You don't hide your thoughts very well," Weston said with a smile.

"Yes, where do we go now?" Sandon asked.

Gavinaugh and Weston looked at Sandon in surprise.

"Penwell is not large enough to contain my enthusiasm. Please let me travel with you, or I think I should wither to nothingness."

"I was hoping as much." Gavinaugh clapped his friend across the back. "Tomorrow we leave for Thecia."

CHAPTER EIGHT

COURT OF
THE LORDS

The road to Thecia was long, hot, and dusty. There were smaller villages along the way that Gavinaugh found it impossible to pass through without proclaiming the Prince. Some of the men from Penwell who were contrary to his words about the Prince had brought testimony to the village leaders against Gavinaugh, and they had stirred up great dissension. On two occasions, he and his companions found it necessary to flee the villages in fear for their lives. Others, however, received Gavinaugh's words with great joy, and more knights were added to the order.

Once in Thecia, Gavinaugh, Weston, Sandon, and Keanna took lodging at an inn not far from the colossal amphitheater that was the centerpiece of the city. Thecia was the largest city they had yet visited, and it was nothing short of marvelous. The architecture of the buildings was spectacular, for the Thecians took great pride in their city. Here the pursuit and preservation of nobility had attained new heights. The social strata of the people were well defined, and they functioned within their estate based almost exclusively on their birth status—nobility, mercantile, or peasant—with no hope of rising beyond the freedoms and rights granted therein.

Since the nobility were at the crest of the social pyramid, all activities were either directly or indirectly performed to serve them. Within the nobility were levels of prestige and power that a knight could actually rise to, given that he possessed excellent skill with the sword and some good fortune. There were various methods by which an aspiring knight could accomplish this. Gallantry and courage on the battlefield were preferred, but battles were not as frequent as nobility required. The natural solution was to provide competitive events among the knights that afforded such opportunities.

Over many years, the prestigious Thecian tournaments evolved into the grand spectacle of the present and provided opportunity for knightly progression within the nobility estate. Many tournaments were held throughout the year in the massive stone amphitheater located at the city's center. People often traveled many days to participate in or observe the games. There were gladiator-style preliminary events where slaves from different regions were forced to battle one another, but the climactic events were the duels between knights of honor.

Gavinaugh and his companions quartered their horses in nearby stables and walked toward the amphitheater where large white columns encircled the outer walls. What was perhaps more impressive was the Court of the Lords near the entrance of the amphitheater. The four were drawn to thirty-two statues arranged in a circle about an elegant pool and fountain that were ornamented with intricate carvings. Each statue stood three times as tall as a man and bore a name in the marble pedestal beneath it. The statues were regal in form, each depicting a powerful man of obvious knighthood. There were also bronze placards affixed beneath the marble carving of each statue with the names of knights and ladies beautifully engraved upon them.

Weston and Sandon were each drawn to various statues, as were Gavinaugh and Keanna. Gavinaugh read each name as he passed: Lord Culverton, Lord Willoughby, Lord Barrington... He stopped at one that caught his attention. It read *The Unknown Lord*. The other statues showed the noble face of each man, but this one's face was covered with a helmet. Gavinaugh also noticed that a brightly colored ribbon with intricate markings was tied about the right foot of each of the other statues, but there was none on this one, and no names of knights or ladies were engraved in its bronze placard.

"This one is different," Keanna said, breaking Gavinaugh's concentration.

"Yes, I wonder why."

"Because no one knows his name," said a young voice behind them.

Gavinaugh and Keanna turned around to see a boy standing near them.

"Who are the other statues of, lad?" Gavinaugh asked.

"Those are the greatest lords that have ever lived in all the kingdom. We honor them with these statues and with the tournaments," the boy replied. "I'm Julian," he said with a broad smile. He looked to be about twelve years old. He set a bundle he was carrying on the ground and put his hand out.

Gavinaugh shook the boy's hand. "I am pleased to meet you, Julian. This is Keanna, and my name is Gavinaugh."

"You're obviously a knight… Are you here to fight in the tournament?" the boy asked.

"No, that is not my intention. Tell me, Julian, why don't they know his name?" Gavinaugh said and motioned to the statue they were standing beneath.

"There is a legend that tells of a great knight who battled a fierce dragon to save a young maiden from being devoured. The dragon was so powerful that all who encountered it were destroyed. But this knight wounded the dragon and freed the young maiden from its lair. He then disappeared without anyone knowing his name. The noblemen of Thecia were fearful to not have a statue in his honor, for it is believed that he will someday return to kill the dragon that still hunts humans by night."

Gavinaugh marveled at the legend and was inspired by the boy's words.

"And what of the ribbons about the ankles of the statues?"

"Oh…those are the ribbons of the mighty knights fighting in the Tournament of Lords tomorrow. This tournament is the grandest of them all and is held only once a year. Each knight chooses one of these great lords to honor at the games as well as a lady from the women of nobility who will be watching. The names of the winning knight and the lady of the tournament are engraved in the bronze placard beneath the lord that is being honored. The highest-ranking knights get to choose first. Lord Culverton is always the first to be selected since he brings the best fortune to the knight who fights for him. Lord Rowland is also a favorite."

Gavinaugh looked around the circle of statues, and his eyes fell once again on the Unknown Lord.

"There isn't a ribbon here. Aren't there enough knights to fight in the tournament?" Gavinaugh asked.

The boy began to laugh. "Hundreds of knights come hoping to fight in the tournament, but none are foolish enough to fight for the Unknown Lord."

"Why not?"

"Because every knight who has ever fought for the Unknown Lord has been defeated in the first round of the tournament," the boy said. "It is believed that there is a curse—if a knight fights for the Unknown Lord and is unworthy, he will be defeated."

Gavinaugh realized that he had the perfect opportunity to gain the attention of the whole city in a day. He looked at Keanna. "May I have the ribbon from your hair?" he asked. She hesitated but yielded the white ribbon to him.

Gavinaugh went to the foot of the statue and tied the ribbon about its ankle.

Julian looked shocked. "But, sir…"

"Julian, how do I let the tournament officials know that I wish to participate?"

"Believe me, Sir Gavinaugh, they already know," the lad replied. "I just hope you don't get killed."

"Killed?" Keanna asked.

"Yes, miss. The knights who fight are often killed, especially if they are unknown in Thecia. At the very least, the losing knight is seriously wounded. Every knight who has ever dared fight for the Unknown Lord has been killed. The last round of the tournament is always to the death. The victor must kill his opponent if he is to be the champion of the tournament. Those are the rules. Thirty-two lords, sixteen contests…so sixteen men will probably die tomorrow, but they will be honored in the Great Hall of Knights. Their names will be carved into the stone wall of the amphitheater to show that they died with honor in the tournaments."

Keanna looked at Gavinaugh and then went to the statue. She reached for the ribbon.

"Miss Keanna, no one is allowed to touch the ribbons once fastened!" Julian sidestepped in her direction. "You will be killed, and the death will be dishonorable."

Keanna stopped, and Gavinaugh gently pulled her hand away from the ribbon.

"It will be all right," he said. He was saddened by the concern on her face, yet he was touched that she cared.

A man dressed in official clothing approached with a quill and parchment. "Your name, sir?"

"I am Sir Gavinaugh of Chessington."

"Chessington? We have not had a knight from Chessington for many years." The man looked at the statue of the Unknown Lord and then back at Gavinaugh. "And I suppose we will not have another for many more," he said as he wrote Gavinaugh's name on the parchment.

"Normally the selection process for admittance into the tournament is stringent, and an unknown knight such as yourself must be recommended by one of the Thecian families of nobility. However, since we have not had a knight fight for the Unknown Lord in many years, I am permitted to make an exception in this case. The entrance fee of twenty florins will still be required *prior* to the tournament tomorrow."

The man raised his chin slightly as if to evaluate Gavinaugh's ability.

"I am certain you will not make it so far as to suffer the humiliation of facing the sword of Sir Bavol," he said, producing a quick, condescending smile. "The first round begins at noon tomorrow. Since you have never participated before, you will want to discuss your obligations with an official prior to the parade at the north gate. A bit of advice…make sure your affairs are in order."

The man turned briskly and left.

"I am sorry, Sir Gavinaugh…I tried to warn you. If you are defeated, you will probably be…" The boy glanced toward Keanna and then lowered his head.

Gavinaugh placed a hand on the lad's shoulder. "Do not fret, lad. The Prince will be with me, and I shall just have to be at my best."

The boy tried to smile but looked sad.

"Who is Sir Bavol?" Gavinaugh asked.

"He has won the last four tournaments. He is a powerful knight. If he wins his fifth tournament, he will be granted the title of lord and receive great honor and wealth. Only one other knight has ever won such an honor, and that was many years ago."

Gavinaugh considered the boy's words as he pondered the highly defined social system within which these people lived. He wondered if they would ever be able to accept the radical new ways of the Prince, for in the King's eyes there was no peasant, merchant, or lord, just people who needed a Deliverer.

"I am late on my errand, sir. Please excuse me. May the lords of Thecia protect you!" He turned toward Keanna and bowed slightly. "Miss," he said and lifted his bundle. He continued on his errand just as Weston and Sandon rejoined Gavinaugh and Keanna.

Keanna turned away and walked to the fountain.

"What was that all about?" Weston asked.

The following morning, there was much pomp and ceremony through-out Thecia. The entire city was caught up in the festivities, from the lords and ladies to the merchants and peasants. The amphitheater would host all of the various tournaments, concluding each day with a round of the Tournament of Lords. It was the climactic event that everyone desired to see.

Gavinaugh went to the north gate early in the morning to see one of the tournament officials. Upon his return, the young lad accompanied him. Weston, Sandon, and Keanna were seated about a table at the inn eating breakfast.

"Julian, this is Sir Weston of Cresthaven and Sir Sandon of Penwell," Gavinaugh said.

The boy bowed.

"And I believe you remember Miss Keanna."

"It is good to see you again, miss."

"Hi, Julian," Keanna said. "How did you happen to find us?"

"I knew Sir Gavinaugh would come to the north gate this morning, so I rose up early and waited there for him," Julian said enthusiastically. "I saw no boy in your service and thought perhaps I could be Sir Gavinaugh's page. The tournament doesn't require it, but I can be very helpful to you. An outsider can quickly get into trouble if he isn't careful."

Sandon laughed. "I think we could use all the help we can get, young Julian. Sir Gavinaugh seems to have an aptitude for getting into trouble wherever he goes."

Keanna handed the boy a plate. "Sit down, Julian, and have some breakfast." She had been unusually quiet since the encounter at the Court of the Lords the previous day, but Julian's presence seemed to help. "Are your parents okay with this?" she asked Julian.

"Yes, Miss Keanna. Sir Gavinaugh has already talked with them," he replied and then set to eating his breakfast.

"What did you learn, Gavinaugh?" Weston asked.

"Names of the knights are drawn today to determine who will be paired for the first round. There are also a number of equestrian events that should not be too difficult. Triumph will do fine."

Weston shook his head. "This is too risky, Gavinaugh. I think you should withdraw. What if you are wounded or killed?"

At Weston's words, all of them stopped eating and stared at Gavinaugh in silence. Gavinaugh considered his words but felt the fervor of his mission rise within him.

"Here is an entire city that has never heard of the Prince. To the Thecians I will be a Thecian that I might win their attention and tell them of the Prince. This opportunity is too great to pass up," he said firmly.

"To withdraw would bring great dishonor, Sir Weston," Julian said humbly. "You would all be cast out of the city. I fear this is all my fault," the boy said and lowered his head.

Keanna put her arm around his shoulder. "Sir Gavinaugh is an excellent knight, Julian. He will be all right," she said quietly, glancing toward Gavinaugh with a stern look that was reminiscent of the glares he had received from her back in Santiok.

Gavinaugh tried to ignore it and turned to Weston and Sandon.

"I do have a bit of a problem, however," Gavinaugh said as he stroked his cheek.

"What is it?" Sandon asked after finishing a bite of his food.

"The tournament requires every knight to have an accompanying squire to handle his horse and weapons. Julian is too young to pass as such."

"The time is too short to find one in the city now," Weston said.

The men returned to eating their meal in silence as they pondered the problem.

"There is only one answer," Sandon said. "I will do it."

"No. I will be your squire," Keanna said firmly.

The men all stared at her. Gavinaugh was stunned that Keanna would offer to serve him as a squire.

"But you are a woman," Sandon said. "I don't think that—"

"I can handle Triumph better than anyone," Keanna interrupted. "And Sir Weston has already given me some training regarding the sword. You are too old to be a squire, and I am able."

Gavinaugh continued to stare at her and then became aware that his expression must have looked rather stupid. He recovered himself.

"Training?" Gavinaugh looked at Weston.

Weston seemed a bit uncomfortable. "At Cresthaven she insisted… she, ah, is quite persistent…and quite good." He smiled at her.

Gavinaugh tried to imagine Keanna wielding a sword but could not see it.

"There is nothing in the rules against it," Julian added.

Gavinaugh looked at Keanna, and she looked at him. Her eyes were a bit softer toward him this time.

"Are you sure?" he asked.

"I am."

"Very well," he said with a nod. "Julian, where can we buy some clothes for her to look the part?"

Before exiting the inn, Gavinaugh took hold of Weston's arm and pulled him aside.

"You trained Keanna with the sword?" he asked.

"She is stronger than she looks, and she has a real aptitude for it," he replied.

Gavinaugh was still amazed, for although he had heard of certain ladies in the past actually fighting in battle, it was an unusual thing.

He turned to leave, but Weston stopped him, looking straight into Gavinaugh's eyes. "I am not as discerning as Marie, but it is clear to me that you care deeply for Keanna."

Gavinaugh looked away. He had not let such thoughts fully materialize in his mind, but Weston spoke what he had felt in his heart for many weeks.

Weston continued. "I don't blame you, Gavinaugh. She is an intriguing woman."

Gavinaugh looked back at his friend. "I can't tell if she likes me or despises me. I just know that for now my duty is to protect her from any further harm."

Weston smiled. "Perhaps that is why she has stayed with us so long…so she can decide. But I don't believe she dislikes you as much as you fear."

Gavinaugh smiled briefly and was encouraged by his words. They turned and left the inn, then joined the others. Before long Keanna was arrayed in the ceremonial garb of a knight in training. She didn't try to hide the fact that she was a young woman. The result was a peculiar but striking personification of beauty and boldness. She wore loose-fitting pants and a colorful blouse beneath a leather doublet. The blue and gold of her garments were a close match to Gavinaugh's armor and banner.

For the tournament, the knights were not allowed full battle armor but only light plate armor that provided minimal protection. They could wear helmets for their entrance into the amphitheater but not during the contests.

Gavinaugh had a squire, a page, and a tournament that would either kill him or give him a platform from which to proclaim the Prince. He knew that his training with the Prince would be as important as the armor he wore, for the men he would be facing in a short time would be more skilled with the sword than any others he had faced. It was a time for vigilance…it was a time for duty.

CHAPTER NINE

TOURNAMENT
OF DEATH

 Keanna was at war within her heart. The factions of her battle were somehow all connected to Gavinaugh. At times she wanted to scream, and at other times she wanted to cry. When she heard Gavinaugh speak of the Prince, she was drawn to the beauty and power of the story. She knew that it was those same words that, if she were to truly embrace them, would require her to offer full forgiveness to Gavinaugh. But part of her wanted to hang on to the bitterness and anger because of what he had done to her and her family months earlier. It was a beast that still reared its ugly head and refused to die.

The irony of it all was that Keanna was strangely drawn to this man who had caused her so much pain. The kindness he now showed her seemed genuine, and she did not deny that there were moments when she wanted to believe it was really true. However, she knew she could not have both vengeance and love, and it seemed as though she would lose her mind in the throes of this conflict. The Prince was calling her to a better place…she just didn't know the way there.

The tournament had forced the silent war within her heart to the forefront of her mind. Deep down she began to understand that she could not hope for his demise, for even the smallest seeds of love had power over the worst of dragons. Her insistence on being Gavinaugh's squire had surprised not only her companions, but herself as well, for the words had passed her lips as though a part of her heart was ruling her tongue—a part that whispered, *He truly cares for you.*

If she could somehow get beyond the clutches of pain and vengeance, she wondered if Gavinaugh's kindness toward her was purely out of remorse and nothing more. She dared not let her heart wander into the fairy tale of love, for she was just a peasant and Gavinaugh had been and always would be a gallant knight.

How could one of his stature ever have feelings for one such as me? she wondered. Such thoughts only added to her confusion and conflict. The only response she could give to Gavinaugh for his attempts at showing her kindness was indifference. Anything else might bring her more pain.

The Tournament of Lords was presided over by the Duke of Thecia and always began with a procession of the thirty-two participating knights riding about the periphery of the amphitheater. Since Gavinaugh was a participant, Weston and Sandon were given respectable seats near the nobility. The nobility seating was near the ground level, distinguishable by double staircases to the left and right of the ceremonial platform. This gave access to the arena for tournament presentations. Vibrant banners decorated the seating area. The duke, along with the marquises, earls, viscounts, barons, and other noblemen and their ladies, were all seated there.

The knights marshaled themselves in an outer court before entering the amphitheater. Keanna made some final adjustments to Triumph's saddle and straightened the colorful horse blanket. Gavinaugh prepared to mount, and Keanna readied the stirrup. He paused and looked at her. He did not understand why she had volunteered to serve as his squire, but he was glad for it. As a Noble Knight, he would not have even dared consider Keanna anything more than just a peasant girl, but here on the other side of his encounter with the Prince, he found exhilarating freedom from such foolishness.

He thought of Leisel in Chessington. According to the estates of the kingdom, she would be an acceptable woman for a knight such as him to court, but it was Keanna who stirred powerful feelings of love in him. For this reason he was all the more grateful for the ways of the Prince. It was the unreachable true nobility of the Prince that demolished the foolishness of social estates among men in Arrethtrae, for the height of a bright star in the heavens looks the same whether gazed upon from a mountain or a valley.

When he did not directly mount Triumph, Keanna looked up at him.

"Keanna...I...," Gavinaugh wanted desperately to share his feelings for her, but he could not find the words. "I am grateful and honored to have you by my side today."

She lowered her head, but he gently lifted up her chin so he could see her eyes.

"You are not my servant...you are my friend," he said.

Keanna's usual countenance of indifference softened, and her eyes seemed to beckon him. Without a single word from her lips, she had completely captured his heart, and he wondered if she even knew it.

Gavinaugh broke the moment for fear of saying something foolish and mounted Triumph. He adjusted his armor, and Keanna handed the reins to him.

"Please don't die today, Sir Gavinaugh," she said quickly and then turned to take her position next to Triumph.

"Knights...forward!" came the command from the front.

The squires each walked beside their mounted knights, who were all arrayed in gleaming armor. Sir Bavol led the procession through an arched gateway to the cheers of thousands of spectators and seemed to revel in the adoration of the crowd. Gavinaugh could hear trumpets ahead heralding the knights' arrival into the arena. He and Keanna were last in the procession, and as they entered, they were amazed at the size of the structure and at the throng of people. Nearly every seat was filled, and Gavinaugh figured over twenty thousand spectators must be present. The bowl shape of the amphitheater captured the voices and added to each subsequent cheer until the noise was constant and nearly deafening. The knights and squires ahead waved to the crowd as their horses pranced about in formation. Triumph seemed to sense the occasion. He held his head high, and his gait became the perfect prance of a show horse.

"They've got nothing on you, Triumph," Keanna said as they watched the riders and horses ahead.

When the procession finished, names were drawn to match opponents. Gavinaugh was pitted against Sir Garamond of Thecia. Theirs would be the final contest of the day. Gavinaugh beckoned Julian. "What do you know of Sir Garamond?" he asked the Thecian lad.

Julian looked quite somber. "He is one of the best in the tournament. It is believed that if any knight could beat Sir Bavol, it would be Sir Garamond."

Keanna, overhearing, looked worried.

Soon the first round of fighting began. Gavinaugh was well acquainted with the gruesome consequences of warfare, but the deaths and injuries that resulted from these duels were senseless, and he could hardly bear to watch. The crowd's cheering made it even worse. He forced himself to watch Sir Bavol's fight, for he presumed he might eventually face him. The crowd cheered loudly for Bavol, and it was clear that he was a favorite. Sir Bavol was indeed a skilled knight, and Gavinaugh recognized the dauntless maneuvers of a man who had tasted real battle many times before. If he should have to face this man, the challenge would be great.

By late afternoon, all of the contests had been fought except Gavinaugh's. Ten men had been killed, and five others were severely wounded. Gavinaugh and Sir Garamond rode from the gates at the opposite ends of the arena through large, ornate stone pillars that extended partway into the fighting area. They turned to salute the duke and the rest of the nobility as the trumpets blew. The herald announced the knights.

"Sir Garamond of Thecia fights to honor Lord Rowland of the Eastern Kingdom!"

The crowd roared with applause and shouts.

"Sir Gavinaugh of Chessington fights to honor"—the herald paused and the crowd hushed to silence—"the Unknown Lord of the Kingdom Beyond!"

A rumble of exclamation and surprise filled the amphitheater. The men dismounted, removed their helmets, and saluted each other. Their squires came to take their horses and helmets. As Gavinaugh handed the reins to Keanna, she looked at him with fear in her eyes.

"It will be all right," he said calmly. She hesitated just a moment and then guided Triumph to the edge of the arena.

The men faced each other, and Gavinaugh looked upon Sir Garamond for the first time. The man's eyes were set like stones in a mighty wall. His jaw was square and his stance powerful. He drew his sword and Gavinaugh followed.

Garamond attacked first, and Gavinaugh countered with a masterful combination. The men exchanged a number of reserved attacks, and Gavinaugh came to admire Garamond's tactics, for they closely matched his own. The exchanges slowly became more and more intense, as did the cheers of the crowd. Each time Garamond advanced, the crowd roared their approval. Each time Gavinaugh advanced, moans of disapproval filled the air.

Garamond was indeed an extremely skilled swordsman, and Gavinaugh suspected that he had not yet seen the man's best. Gavinaugh countered a slice and initiated a steady combination of power and speed that put Garamond in retreat as their blades of steel collided time after time. It was aggressive but certainly not indicative of Gavinaugh's full reserve of skill. Gavinaugh halted his attack and looked into his opponent's eyes, questioning the man's level of confidence. Garamond's eyes had widened slightly, and Gavinaugh could sense his realization that he was facing something he had never faced before.

Garamond did not hesitate long, however, and charged full ahead with a set of cuts and slices that was a challenge for Gavinaugh to thwart. He countered and retreated, but then held his ground. The distance between them closed. Garamond brought a cut from the left. Gavinaugh blocked it, spun, and brought a slice across Garamond's chest that tore into his armor. He stumbled backward, and Gavinaugh executed a thrust that passed between Garamond's chest and right arm. The men were nearly chest to chest, and for an instant they locked eyes. Garamond's expression was one of wonder, for Gavinaugh had executed his thrust purposefully off target to miss the man's chest.

"Your fight is noble. The Unknown Lord would be honored," Gavinaugh said.

The men parted and Garamond seemed momentarily stunned.

"Garamond…Garamond…Garamond…" The crowd began to chant, and Garamond's face was set once again to the fight.

Garamond exploded with such massive blows and speed that Gavinaugh knew they were the extent of all he had. Gavinaugh labored to quell the attack. In the midst of the advance, he feigned retreat, ducked beneath a high cut, predicted Garamond's next move, and brought a powerful counterblow that nearly knocked Garamond's sword from his grip.

In that moment, the euphoria of the crowd dwindled to exclamations of surprise as Gavinaugh unleashed a volley of rapid blows that Garamond could not repel. Garamond's countenance became as one who had awakened a sleeping tiger. His retreat was inevitable as he narrowly deflected slice after slice. In one massive, circling cut, Gavinaugh's blade blasted into Garamond's and sent his sword flying many paces away. He fell backward and onto the ground, exhausted and defeated. Gavinaugh quickly covered Garamond and stood over him with his sword raised high for the final thrust. The crowd fell silent as they realized that one of their best had been defeated by an unknown knight fighting for the Unknown Lord. It was a historical event that brought every spectator in the stadium to his feet, including the Duke of Thecia.

"Death with honor!" shouted various people from the crowd until the stadium reverberated with the chant.

Gavinaugh scanned the stadium and then looked deep into Garamond's eyes. The man closed his eyes and prepared for his final breath. Gavinaugh raised his sword a little higher and then plunged the gleaming steel blade deep into the soil beside Garamond's chest.

The crowd fell into an eerie silence once again. Garamond opened his eyes.

"Sir Gavinaugh of Chessington!" the master tournament official called out. "You must either kill or disable your opponent to advance in the tournament. If you do not, you forfeit your right in the next round."

Gavinaugh pulled his sword from the ground and held it before him.

"Nobility and citizens of Thecia!" Gavinaugh called loudly for all to hear. "Sir Garamond fought a noble and honorable fight. His death would serve no purpose. Never before has a knight fought for the Unknown Lord in your tournament and lived. This same Lord requires of me to spare this man's life. If that means I don't advance, then so be it, for I will honor my Lord before you. If you should choose to eliminate me from the tournament, let it be known that the victor of your tournament will not have defeated the knight who fights for the Unknown Lord, and your champion will be no champion at all!"

A moment of uncertainty flashed across the official's face, and the murmurings of the crowd grew in volume. Another official came to talk with the first. A moment later they ascended the staircases to the nobility and conferred with the Duke of Thecia.

In the commotion, Gavinaugh knelt down to his fallen opponent and grabbed his hand.

"Rise up, Sir Garamond, and do not be ashamed. The Prince of Arrethtrae has need of you in life much more so than in death," Gavinaugh said. He lifted Garamond from the arena floor, and the man stared at him in astonishment.

"No matter the outcome of this day, Sir Gavinaugh, know that I will serve you as my liege…I so swear!" Garamond spoke with passion and knelt before him.

"No, Garamond. Rise up and do not serve me. Serve the Prince of this kingdom, who came to save us all," Gavinaugh said as he lifted Garamond once more to his feet.

"Tell me who this Prince is that deserves the devotion of a knight as noble as you, and I shall follow Him to the ends of the kingdom."

Gavinaugh smiled and placed his hand on Garamond's shoulder. "That I shall, for His kingdom is reserved for hearts such as yours, my friend."

"Gavinaugh of Chessington!" shouted the tournament official. The crowd hushed to hear the judgment of the duke.

"By the grace of the Duke of Thecia and in honor of the Unknown Lord, you are allowed to advance. Any further infractions of tournament rules, however, will not be tolerated!"

The crowd roared their approval, and the ovation did not diminish for a long while.

Gavinaugh bowed to the duke to show his appreciation. The squires returned with their steeds, and the two men and their escorts exited the amphitheater.

Garamond invited Gavinaugh, Weston, Sandon, Keanna, and Julian to dine with him that evening at his manor. After an elaborate meal of the finest foods Thecia had to offer, Gavinaugh shared the story of the

Prince with Garamond. He listened intently and seemed nearly over-whelmed by the words.

"I have searched the kingdom over for a cause noble enough to dedicate my life to and found nothing worthy. These words you speak ignite a fire in my heart that the Great Sea itself could not quench. From this day forward I will serve this Prince you speak of and the King who reigns from a distant land."

Gavinaugh knighted Garamond as a Knight of the Prince, and another companion soul joined the army of the Prince.

Garamond insisted that his new friends stay with him while in Thecia, for his manor was large and had many rooms. He shared all that he owned with them, as well as his knowledge of the knights Gavinaugh would face in the days to come. They were all very grateful.

The following day, Gavinaugh faced his next opponent, and the fight was over quickly, for his skill far surpassed that of the other knight. Once again he refused to kill him, and the officials had a mind to eliminate him. By now, however, Gavinaugh had become a favorite of the crowd, and the influence of their cheers was too much to overcome, so he was allowed to advance without even a warning.

Each day Gavinaugh fought and was victorious until only one knight remained for him to defeat—Sir Bavol of Whighton.

Word of the mighty Sir Gavinaugh, who fought for the Unknown Lord, had spread not only through all of Thecia, but throughout the surrounding regions. On the last day of the tournament, the seats, the aisles, and the gates were all crowded with bystanders hoping to see the final contest. Distant thunder rumbled as the sky threatened to release its rain from the dark clouds above, but Thecia and its citizens did not care—the excitement of this event overshadowed the discomforts of any possible inclement weather.

Under the north gate to the amphitheater, Weston, Sandon,

Garamond, Keanna, and Julian readied Gavinaugh and Triumph both, for the final duel was to be fought on horseback.

"I have watched Sir Bavol for two years and dared not enter the tournament before now because of him," Garamond said as he secured Gavinaugh's breastplate. "He is not only very skilled, but deceptive besides. The mounted duel is his forte, and you will be at a disadvantage since you are left-handed."

Gavinaugh's five friends stood before him, and he could read the concern on each of their faces. He smiled broadly at them all.

"What do you find so humorous, Gavinaugh?" Weston asked, a bit perturbed.

"I have never had so much fuss over me in all of my days as a knight," he said with a laugh as he mounted Triumph. "I think I shall have to find more tournaments to fight in." His humor seemed to ease the tension.

"May the Lords of—" Garamond stopped himself. "May the Prince be with you!"

"And with you!" Gavinaugh replied.

Weston, Sandon, and Garamond made their way to the seats that were reserved for them near the nobility as Keanna walked beside Gavinaugh into the amphitheater at the sound of the trumpets and to the deafening roar of twenty-five thousand cheering spectators.

Bavol entered from the south gate and raised his hand to accept the adoration of thousands. He was a powerful-looking knight with jet-black hair and a beard to match. His steed was two hands taller than Triumph, which added to his dominating stature. When Gavinaugh saw that many were shouting his own name, he stopped Triumph near the towering stone pillars and began to dismount.

"What are you doing?" Keanna asked, alarmed at his actions.

He continued to dismount. "It is wrong for these people to lift any man other than the Prince up like this," he replied, walking beside Keanna to the center of the arena.

Along the way, Keanna kept looking over at Gavinaugh, as though she could hardly believe he would do such a thing.

At the arena center, Gavinaugh left Triumph and walked Keanna to the side of the arena, and the cheers of the crowd subsided into a rumble of muttered conversations.

"Thank you for all you have done to help me over the past few days," Gavinaugh said.

Keanna opened her mouth to speak but could not form any words. The crowd hushed as Gavinaugh bowed to her and then returned to Triumph. The reaction from the people and the nobility was clearly one of confusion and amazement.

When Gavinaugh reached his steed, he mounted and prepared for the fight. The herald announced the knights, and they separated for their mounted passes. Each man drew his sword, and the trumpet sounded.

The men charged full speed toward one another, their gleaming blades before them. Gavinaugh could feel his mighty Triumph pounding the ground beneath but could not hear it, for the shouts of the crowd flooded the amphitheater and overwhelmed all other sounds. Since the injury to his right arm years before, Gavinaugh hadn't been in battle with Triumph and so didn't know how the horse would respond to his being left-handed. But the steed seemed to understand his limitation.

At the final moment, Triumph crossed over before Bavol's horse, and Gavinaugh was able to strike a forceful blow upon Bavol's breastplate that nearly sent him to the ground. Bavol cursed and recovered quickly. He positioned his horse to regain his right-side advantage, but

Triumph instinctively repositioned himself for Gavinaugh's advantage time and time again. Bavol's frustration was obvious as he tried to engage Gavinaugh across his body. Gavinaugh took advantage of Triumph's brilliant maneuvering and landed blow after blow upon Bavol.

At one point, Gavinaugh saw an opening in Bavol's guard and brought a wide, powerful slice across his body. Bavol's only response was to bring his sword up just in time to stop what would have been a deadly cut across his neck and chest. The clash was near the hilt and so strong, however, that Bavol's sword broke in two. Bavol cursed again and threw the shattered remnants of his sword to the ground as he galloped to his squire to receive a new sword.

The thunder from the sky was replaced by the thunder of spectators pounding their feet upon the stone steps of the amphitheater. The sky began to break, letting spires of sunlight through the dark clouds.

Bavol turned from his squire and charged ferociously at Gavinaugh again, but this time he hesitated at the engagement and drove his horse right into Triumph. As the horses collided, Bavol lunged at Gavinaugh, and horses and men all fell to the ground in a heap of clashing armor and flailing hooves. Gavinaugh rolled away from the fracas, hoping that Triumph was all right. He began to stand, but out of the corner of his eye he caught the shadow of a deadly blade arching toward his head. He brought his sword into a protective position above and behind him in time to stop Bavol's cut. Bavol recoiled and struck again, but Gavinaugh ducked, turned, and executed a quick and shallow thrust that penetrated Bavol's thigh just above his plate armor. Gavinaugh then fully recovered to a standing defensive position.

Both men were breathing heavily. To Gavinaugh, Bavol looked angry and frustrated. The injury to Bavol's thigh did not appear to hinder the man at all, however, and he attacked Gavinaugh in a steady advance of cuts and slices. Gavinaugh was momentarily taken by the strength of Bavol's blows and tried to adjust. This knight was one of the best Gavinaugh had ever faced, and for a moment he wondered if he would survive the day. The crowd had worked itself into a near-frenzied state during the course of the fight, and Gavinaugh found it difficult to concentrate. Bavol's energy and attack seemed endless as his blade pounded into Gavinaugh's. One of Bavol's cuts was so strong that it slammed into Gavinaugh's sword and continued into his shoulder. His shoulder plate bore the brunt of the blow, but Bavol's sword glanced off and hit his head just above his ear.

He could feel the blood oozing down his neck as he made a gallant effort to recover. The crowd shouted wildly. Gavinaugh continued his retreat from Bavol's tireless attack, which put him up against one of the stone pillars. Bavol made a massive two-handed crosscut that crashed into Gavinaugh's sword. Gavinaugh could not maintain his grip as his weapon tore loose from his hand. He stepped backward in retreat and tripped over a corner of the foundation block the pillar was set upon. Gavinaugh was lying on his back without his sword. The crowd quieted as Bavol covered him and raised his sword for the final deathblow.

Gavinaugh glanced toward Keanna, who was just below the seating for nobility. She had fallen to her knees and covered her face with her hands. All the kingdom seemed to stop, and the next moment stalled its arrival. Gavinaugh thought of the Prince and the compassion He had shown him. *How foolish to end my mission in a way such as this!* Gavinaugh saw Bavol's sword descending from above in a two-handed plunge, but strangely, he was not afraid. His mind had transitioned to a state he had never experienced before.

The blade came down, and Gavinaugh rolled just far enough for it to miss its mark. He rolled back and grabbed on to the hilt of Bavol's sword with his left hand. Bavol pulled his sword upward and away for another strike, but Gavinaugh held tightly to the hilt, using the movement to lift him from the ground. He was catapulted to a standing position and carried his momentum forward. He swung his right elbow forward with all his might into Bavol's jaw, and the blow sent the man reeling backward. Gavinaugh made use of the time to recover his sword and faced Bavol once again.

"You have only prolonged your death!" Bavol shouted as he rubbed his jaw and prepared to attack again.

The cheering of the crowd was once again deafening, but this time Gavinaugh did not hear them. He had discovered the strength of the Prince, and there was no one who could strip him of that power. He took a swordsman's stance that portrayed his renewed confidence and viewed the coming fight with anticipation.

Bavol attacked as before, but this time Gavinaugh did not retreat. His blade flew faster and more accurately than ever, and his domination in the fight was undeniable. He began a methodical advance and realized that he could take Bavol down in an instant—he was relying completely upon the training he had received from the Prince. He did not want to kill Bavol, but he knew that the man would not submit until his last breath.

Bavol's countenance of assurance changed to one of desperation as he seemed to realize the shift of momentum in the fight.

Gavinaugh paused in his attack. "Yield, Sir Bavol, or you will surely die."

The men were breathing heavily, and sweat ran down their faces and bodies. There was now more sun than shade, for the clouds in the sky were few.

"It is you who will die this day!" Bavol lunged forward and attacked, but Gavinaugh anticipated the move, deflected his cut, and plunged his sword through Bavol's right arm. Bavol screamed but did not drop his sword. He transferred it to his left hand and attacked again. Gavinaugh defended and made a thrust into Bavol's shoulder. Before long, Bavol was bleeding from multiple wounds, but he would not yield.

Bavol attempted a final weak attack, but Gavinaugh easily deflected the cut and quickly followed with a blow that Bavol could not defend. The swords collided and Bavol lost his grip. His sword flew from his hand, and Gavinaugh advanced to prevent him from recovering it. Bavol grabbed his right arm to staunch the blood flowing freely from the wound. There was no fight left in him. The crowd erupted into an ovation that did not subside.

Bavol fell to his knees before Gavinaugh. "You must kill me to end my shame," he said weakly.

The crowd began to yell, "Death with honor!"

Gavinaugh turned to the seats of the nobility and held up his hand to quiet the people. After a moment, all were silent as they waited for Gavinaugh to finish the contest and become the champion of the Tournament of Lords.

"People of Thecia, why do you need the death of a man to make a champion victorious?" he shouted. He turned so as to talk to everyone in the amphitheater. "Let me tell you about the death of a Champion who made His *Followers* victorious! I fight for the Unknown Lord. You have ignorantly given honor to Him through the statue in the Court of the Lords, yet you do not know Him. I have seen Him and will testify before all of Arrethtrae that He is nobler than any lord in any land, for He is the Son of the King and the Prince of Arrethtrae. By Him was this kingdom established, and through Him this kingdom will be saved. He came to teach us of the King and of the Code, but for the truth He spoke, He was hung upon a tree. People, hear and believe this—He is now alive, for I have seen Him face-to-face, and there is none like Him in the entire kingdom."

Gavinaugh turned and looked down at Bavol. "There is no shame in losing to the sword of the Prince. There is only shame in choosing not to follow Him."

Bavol looked as though he were about to fall, for his wounds were beginning to overcome him. Gavinaugh motioned to Bavol's squire just as the knight fell sideways. Gavinaugh grabbed him and gently laid him on the ground. His squire and two other men came to help.

Bavol looked into Gavinaugh's face and grabbed his arm. "Tell me of the ways of the Unknown Lord that I may teach them to my people at Whighton." Bavol's words were strained.

"I will, good knight, and you will have reward a thousand times that of this tournament!" he said, inspired by the heart of the man. He stood and allowed the other men to care for Bavol.

The Duke of Thecia rose from his chair. The tournament officials motioned for the crowd to hush again.

"Sir Gavinaugh of Chessington," the duke said loudly. "Your words about the Unknown Lord are strange to us, but we cannot deny your skill or your victory this day. You are indeed champion of the Tournament of Lords!"

The crowd gave a riotous ovation that could not be easily quieted. After some time, the duke spoke again.

"Come and choose a lady from the nobility upon which to bestow the honor of Lady of the Tournament of Lords."

The duke motioned to the ladies seated about him. There were many beautiful and dignified ladies. Those who had received such an honor before wore pendants signifying such. The master tournament official came and guided Gavinaugh up one of the staircases and onto the ceremonial platform. The duke presented him with a pendant and a royal robe that he was to bequeath to the chosen lady. The pendant was bright gold with a ruby set amid intricate inlays. The robe was as exquisite a garment as Gavinaugh had ever seen, made of red velvet with white lace edgings. The collar was cream colored silk that shined like the moon off the still Crimson River.

Gavinaugh looked into the faces of the women. Some sat with a dignified look of propriety, while others seemed to beg with their eyes to be chosen. Two nights before the tournament began, there had been a ball where the knights and ladies were to become acquainted, but Gavinaugh's late arrival and selection for the tournament had caused him to miss the affair. He was thankful, for being in the presence of the Thecian nobility felt like being back in the world of the Noble Knights.

He looked out into the faces of the common people and thought of the Prince. The Prince had not chosen the Noble Knights; He had chosen peasants. And Gavinaugh had seen more nobility in the hearts of those peasants than he had ever seen in the upper estates. And beyond that, the Prince had now chosen the Outdwellers since the people of Chessington had rejected Him.

Gavinaugh folded the robe over his right arm and held the pendant in his hand. He walked down the staircase away from the nobility.

"Sir Gavinaugh, you must choose a lady," the duke said sternly.

Gavinaugh paused midway down the staircase. "I shall, good sir."

The crowd began to murmur. They had never seen a knight so boldly cast aside the traditions of men.

Gavinaugh continued down the staircase and walked toward Keanna. As he approached, she stepped aside to let him pass, but he did not pass by. He faced her and looked into her eyes—eyes filled with wonder and puzzlement. He held out his left arm for her, but she backed away, shaking her head.

"Keanna, in the eyes of the King we are all equal—there is neither nobleman nor peasant. What He sees are people who need a Deliverer. When we accept that, we become royalty, like His Son. You may consider yourself a peasant, but the King sees a princess...and so do I."

Keanna stared blankly at Gavinaugh and then lowered her head. Since he had never expressed his feelings to her before, he wondered if such words might rekindle the animosity she had previously felt for him. She looked back up at him, and he saw that her eyes were moist. She slowly took his arm, and they proceeded up the staircase. There was great commotion in the crowd. On the platform, Gavinaugh took the royal robe and placed it upon Keanna's shoulders. He then fastened the pendant about her neck. She turned to face Gavinaugh, and he was taken once again with her beauty.

Gavinaugh addressed the awestruck crowd. "The Prince I spoke of is coming again to rule in honor and in truth. Open your eyes and believe, for He calls each of you, whether noble or peasant. He cares not of the stature of a man but of the condition of his heart. All are equal in the eyes of the Prince!"

Gavinaugh turned to face Keanna, bowed deeply to her, and then proclaimed, "I present to you, Lady Keanna of Arrethtrae…Lady of the Tournament of Lords!"

The applause was slow to begin, but as it started with the common people, it spread quickly. Within a few moments, there was an ovation mixed with shouts that shook the stadium. Even the nobility eventually joined, for they looked foolish to remain still.

Gavinaugh held his hand out to Keanna, and she slipped her hand in his. Though soiled by the dust of the arena, the warmth of his touch seemed to flow up her arm and fill her heart. She could no longer deny the strong feelings she had for him. When Gavinaugh nearly died during the battle against Bavol, she felt as though she would die herself. The feelings she had suppressed were laid bare by the threat of his death, and her heart pleaded with the King to save him. Now, in the presence of twenty-five thousand, he had lifted her from peasantry to nobility in an instant.

The roar of the crowd continued to fill the amphitheater, and Keanna didn't know how to respond to such a thing. At first she was horribly embarrassed and wanted to disappear, but the response from the crowd was overwhelming, and soon she could not help the tears that spilled onto her cheeks as she looked about the amphitheater. The tears she shed watered the seeds of forgiveness in her heart. They cast the beast of vengeance away. They healed the wounds of anguish. They welcomed the hope of love. Lady Keanna had arrived, and it was all because of the Prince.

Gavinaugh held her hand and turned her to face the people. Her hand felt delicate in his, and he sensed no hurry from her to abandon his touch. They descended the stairs, and he called for Triumph. He readied himself to lift her onto Triumph's back, but she hesitated and looked at him. She smiled through her tears, reached up, and gently kissed his cheek. He felt forgiven all over again and thought his heart might leap from his chest. He lifted her onto Triumph and then walked beside her, leading Triumph toward the north gate. All the while, the cheers of the crowd did not diminish.

This Tournament of Lords would not be easily forgotten by the people of Thecia, for a Knight of the Prince had come to proclaim His work among the Outdwellers and bring true nobility within reach of the common people.

CHAPTER TEN

OLD MASTER

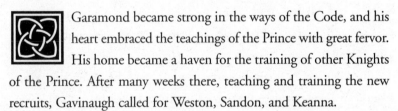Garamond became strong in the ways of the Code, and his heart embraced the teachings of the Prince with great fervor. His home became a haven for the training of other Knights of the Prince. After many weeks there, teaching and training the new recruits, Gavinaugh called for Weston, Sandon, and Keanna.

"It is time to return to Chessington," Gavinaugh said.

Sandon and Keanna did not fully understand what this meant, but Weston did.

"That is not wise, Gavinaugh," he said. "You know that Kifus and the Noble Knights would love nothing better than for you to go to Chessington. At Cresthaven, I met with Sir Nias, and he assured me that Kifus's desire to find you is greater than ever, especially since your fame is spreading throughout the kingdom. If you go to Chessington, you can expect to hang."

Weston spoke more strongly than Gavinaugh had ever heard, and Sandon and Keanna were obviously disturbed by his words.

"I appreciate your concern, Weston, but you cannot persuade me otherwise. I must meet with our fellow knights there, and if perchance I should meet with Kifus, then so be it. His sword is no more deadly than any others we have faced. The Prince will be with us."

Weston did not look pleased, and although there was great division in their thinking, the three Knights of the Prince and Keanna prepared for their journey to the center of the kingdom…Chessington!

On the day of their departure, many difficult farewells were made, especially the one with Julian.

"It is an honor to have served you, Sir Gavinaugh," Julian said stoically, trying to hide the quiver in his voice.

Gavinaugh knelt down and placed a hand on the lad's shoulder.

"The honor is mine, young knight," Gavinaugh said and gazed deeply into the bright eyes of the boy. "And I am as certain as the sunrise that we will one day hear of the mighty deeds of a gallant knight who serves the Prince with his whole heart… Arrethtrae awaits you, Sir Julian, Knight of the Prince!"

Julian's face beamed his appreciation, and he threw his arms around Gavinaugh's neck. Gavinaugh returned the embrace until Julian seemed to sense a need to be more professional again. He retreated a step and bowed. Gavinaugh stood and smiled broadly at the lad, then allowed the others a chance to say farewell.

After many days of traveling, they came to the city of Chessington by night and met with Cedric, William, Rob, Barrett, and many other mighty Knights of the Prince. For days they shared their tales of adventure and how the Prince and His Silent Warriors had protected and guided them every step of the way.

Gavinaugh was overjoyed to share how the Prince was transforming lives throughout the kingdom. The havens and the Knights of the Prince were multiplying and growing stronger in many cities, and Gavinaugh felt replenished by the spirit of knightly brotherhood. Though the kingdom seemed to groan at the silent war that raged for its future, there was a Camelot in the hearts of the knights that could not be destroyed even if Lucius unleashed his entire arsenal of evil upon them. They all felt humbled to have been called by the Prince for such a time as this. From the lowest pauper to the wealthiest nobleman, all were brothers in the army of the Prince. As the training of the knights continued, the needs of all were met by the abundance of many.

Gavinaugh remained in Chessington with the knights for many weeks. Weston returned to Cresthaven to his family, and Keanna and Sandon found opportunities to serve the Followers in many ways during their stay.

Gavinaugh sensed an entirely different atmosphere in the streets of Chessington. At first he thought perhaps it was his dramatic change of perspective, but eventually he came to realize that this was not the case. The arrival of the Prince had initiated a transformation of social and political structure that the Noble Knights could not stop, though they desperately fought to do so. Gavinaugh had felt it when he was a Noble Knight seeking to destroy the Followers, and now it became obvious to him what it was. The order of the Noble Knights was dying. It was early, like the nagging, deep cough of a man who hasn't yet realized that he has contracted a deadly disease, but it was an eventuality.

Gavinaugh suspected that the Noble Knights themselves might not have realized it, but their desperation was becoming more and more obvious. On the whole, the people of Chessington had not accepted the Prince as the true Son of the King and were, in fact, more antagonistic toward the Knights of the Prince than ever. However, despite their resistance, they had seen true nobility personified by the Prince, and as a result, the glory of the Noble Knights seemed to fade with each passing day. As the Noble Knights lost the respect of the people, they also lost their purpose. An order of knights without purpose or a noble cause dies. And the danger with a dying man is the desperate measures he will take to stay alive—even if his death is inevitable. Gavinaugh feared what the Noble Knights might do…

Gavinaugh's secret return was eventually revealed, and Kifus and the Noble Knights began to plot and search. Not all his ties with the Noble Knights had been severed, however—two knights had come to believe in the Prince and had remained to be the eyes and ears for the Knights of the Prince. As a result, Gavinaugh was always a step ahead of the fetters that bore his name, and Kifus's frustration mounted.

One day Gavinaugh was training a group of new recruits on the outskirts of the city while Cedric, William, and the others were occupied with establishing a new haven not far from Chessington. Keanna had just brought some water for the knights when they were interrupted by an urgent voice.

"Gavinaugh!" Sandon ran to him from across the hill. Gavinaugh was alarmed, for he had never seen Sandon approach in such a rush.

"Gavinaugh!" he shouted again as he reached him. Sandon was out of breath and could hardly stand straight as he struggled to get his words out. His eyes were wide and filled with panic.

"What is it, Sandon?" Gavinaugh asked, impatient for him to catch his breath.

"In the square"—Sandon gasped—"Kifus is hanging a man."

He took another deep breath and grabbed Gavinaugh's arms. "It is Weston. They have captured Weston and are going to hang him."

Gavinaugh ran to Triumph, and Sandon followed. As Gavinaugh mounted, Sandon seized Triumph's bridle and tried to speak his final words.

"Kifus has Weston's family too. He's going to hang them all!"

"No!" Keanna looked frantically for a horse to mount.

"Keanna, stay here!" Gavinaugh said. He saw Sandon mounting a horse, but he did not wait. He pulled on the reins to set Triumph's direction and bolted toward the city square.

The sweet faces of Marie, Addy, and Keaton filled Gavinaugh's mind. He was overwhelmed by powerful emotions of anger and love. Triumph ran faster than he had ever run before, but it was not enough for Gavinaugh. With each passing moment he wondered if he would be too late. The shops on the streets flew by in a blur, and his anger toward Kifus became great. He approached the square, and Triumph leaped over the stone wall that bordered the east side.

Many people were gathered, and the entire force of Noble Knights encircled the large oak tree where Weston, Marie, Addy, and Keaton sat atop horses, with ropes about their necks. A Noble Knight stood beside Weston's horse, waiting for the command to slap the animal and end his life.

Gavinaugh became enraged. *"Kifus!"* Gavinaugh shouted while still some distance away. *"Kifus!"*

The crowd's focus shifted from the tree to Gavinaugh. He drew his sword, and the people separated to let him through. His approach was so fierce that even the Noble Knights hesitated. Gavinaugh dismounted and bounded toward Kifus. Many knights reached for their swords, but Kifus motioned for them to stand down. Kifus stood near Weston with his arms crossed, a smug smile on his face.

Sandon arrived just behind Gavinaugh, but a dozen knights quickly overtook him and held him captive.

Gavinaugh looked at Weston, whose face was badly beaten. Marie, Addy, and Keaton were silent, but tears streamed down their faces. It was more than Gavinaugh could bear, for he knew that they were experiencing this moment of terror because they had shown kindness to him.

"I was told these people are important to you," Kifus said delightedly. "Now I know just how important."

"Let them go, Kifus, or my sword will cut through every Noble Knight here until I reach your throat!"

Kifus's smile vanished, and wrath filled its place. He drew his sword, and the men slowly began to circle each other.

"I have been looking forward to this for a very long time," Kifus said angrily. "You were my best, Gavin. I gave you my trust...I gave you my honor…I gave you my sister…and you have become a traitor to all. The traitor you helped me kill has poisoned you, and now you are an enemy of Chessington!"

"Look around you, Kifus," Gavinaugh said. "The kingdom is embracing the truth of the Prince, and you can't stop it. You speak of honor, but you have resorted to killing children!" He pointed to Addy and Keaton. "The order of the Noble Knights is dying, and your desperate attempt to keep it alive is never more evident than what we see here today. As I was, you have now become—a tool of the Dark Knight!"

Kifus yelled and attacked. Their swords met with the ferocity of two tigers battling to the death.

"You never could defeat me before, Gavin, and now you fight left-handed. Not only are you a traitor, but you have also become a fool."

"A fool for the Prince is better than a hero for Lucius," Gavinaugh rebutted, and his words fueled another onslaught of powerful blows.

The crowd watched in astonishment as Gavinaugh thwarted every attack Kifus initiated. With the exception of the stranger, Kifus had never been defeated. Gavinaugh experienced the best Kifus had and began to advance with the power and speed he had learned from the Prince. The fight turned in Gavinaugh's favor, and Kifus struggled to maintain control—Gavinaugh could see the anxiety in his eyes.

Kifus renewed his fight and nearly landed a deadly thrust, but Gavinaugh thwarted it at the last moment. He then brought a heavy crosscut that Kifus only partly deflected, and the blade sliced his chin and then tore into his breastplate. Kifus retreated, blood spilling from his chin through his fingers. Victory for Gavinaugh was now just a matter of time, and Kifus seemed to fully understand it. He looked at Gavinaugh with renewed hate and then turned to the knight beside Weston.

"Hang them!" he said and pointed to Weston with his sword.

Before Gavinaugh could react, the knight slapped the horse. Weston's face contorted into the pained visage of impending death as the rope jerked tight. Marie screamed, and the children cried as they witnessed the execution attempt of their father. The crowd gasped, and Gavinaugh could hear Sandon scream in protest.

Gavinaugh could hardly believe the nightmare unfolding before him. "Triumph—to Weston!" he shouted. He then turned upon Kifus with such fury that a legion of knights would not have been able to stay his sword.

Triumph quickly whisked beneath Weston and gave him his back to relieve the suffocating strain of the rope. The knight guarding Weston attempted to stop the horse, but Triumph ignored him. The man slapped his hindquarter, but Triumph quickly turned his hind legs to the knight and kicked him. The knight flew ten paces and remained motionless on the ground.

Kifus had no defense against the mastery of Gavinaugh's sword. With the speed of lightning, Gavinaugh blasted Kifus's sword from his hand. Before other Noble Knights could come to his aid, Kifus was pinned against the tree with Gavinaugh's sword pressed against his throat.

"Release them, Kifus, or I will finish this cut!"

"You will die too, traitor," Kifus said, straining against the razor-sharp edge of the sword.

Gavinaugh looked into Kifus's eyes and felt the rage coursing through his veins. "Do not be a fool, Kifus," Gavinaugh said. "We both know that I am already a dead man. You, however, can choose to save your life by sparing theirs. Choose quickly, for my patience with you is gone!"

The Noble Knights had all drawn their swords and were awaiting Kifus's bidding. He hesitated to answer.

"I have who I want," he said with a wry smile. "Release them."

Once Weston's family had been released, Weston and Sandon hesitated to leave Gavinaugh in such a hopeless predicament.

"Go!" he commanded.

Gavinaugh did not release his grip on Kifus until Sandon, Weston,

Marie, and the children were far beyond the square. Once he dropped his sword, the Noble Knights descended on Gavinaugh harshly, but they saved the brunt of their brutality for later, out of the sight of the citizens of Chessington. Gavinaugh was beaten and cast into the prison that he himself had once filled with Followers.

He felt the cold steel of the prison bars and remembered his first encounter with William. It lifted his despair, for he would not trade sides of the prison bars for all the gold in the kingdom if it meant giving up the Prince. His face was bruised and his brow was bleeding, but he was free and he was healed. No man could take that from him.

That evening, Leisel came to Gavinaugh in the prison and commanded the guard to leave them. She looked into the cell, and he rose to greet her.

"Hello, fair Leisel," he said tenderly.

At his words, her sober countenance softened to one of heartache.

"Gavin, why did you do this? I could have made you happy. We could have been together and made a paradise to live in. Didn't you ever care for me?" Leisel clutched the bars that separated them.

Gavinaugh came close to Leisel and put his hands on hers. He looked into her eyes. "Yes, Leisel, I did."

For a moment she looked hopefully into his face. "It isn't too late, Gavin!" she said, but then stopped and gazed at him. "But I can see in your eyes that you have since given your heart to another."

Leisel turned her head away and withdrew her hands from his. "Is she pretty?"

Gavinaugh did not answer, for he could not be so cruel.

"Is she nobility, perhaps a princess?" She began to cry.

"Leisel, the Prince came first to the people of Chessington…to people like us. But we refused Him. He desires for you to follow Him, and so do I," he said.

"What does that imposter have to do with you and me?" she asked, wiping away her tears.

"Everything, Leisel! The Prince breaks the bonds of slavery and lifts the peasant to nobility."

Leisel looked disgusted and walked away from him. She turned around abruptly. "What has happened to you? You were the pride of Chessington…Gavin, the mighty Noble Knight. Now look at you!" She motioned with her hand to remind him of the prison he was in.

"I met the Prince, and He restored my broken soul," Gavinaugh said. "He makes things new, Leisel, and He is calling you too. All you have to do is listen and follow." Gavinaugh hurt for Leisel. She was a prisoner behind the bars of religious devotion to a false concept of nobility.

"I had to come and see for myself if what they said of you was true, but it is worse than I had imagined." Leisel straightened her back and walked with an air of dignity toward the stairs that exited the prison. She turned toward him one last time.

"Good-bye, Gavin. Enjoy your foolish new life, for I will have no part of it or of you."

"Good-bye, fair Leisel," he said softly, but she did not hear him. Her elegant gown flowed about her slender form as she ascended the stone steps and exited the prison chamber.

CHAPTER ELEVEN

A KNIGHT'S FAREWELL

 Two days before the official trial in the Great Hall, Kifus commanded that Gavinaugh be brought to him in his private chamber. Gavinaugh stood before him, not as a man who had been beaten and imprisoned—although the fetters were still securely fastened about his limbs—but as a man at peace with his heart. The contentment on his face seemed to anger Kifus, who looked away and took a deep breath, apparently to quash his anger. When he looked back at Gavinaugh, there was genuine pity on his face.

Kifus turned to the guard who had accompanied Gavinaugh. "Remove his chains and leave us."

The guard looked questioningly at Kifus and then complied.

Kifus stared at Gavinaugh. "Why, Gavin?"

It was a simple question, but it revealed much to Gavinaugh. "Please don't think me insolent if I first ask a question of you before I answer."

Kifus nodded.

"Why do you want to know?" Gavinaugh asked.

Kifus was silent for a moment. "Because I loved you as a son, and I knew you to be a man of honor, integrity, and loyalty. Of all the Noble Knights I have served and who have served under me, I would not have expected you to betray our cause. That is why. I need to know how such a thing could happen to one of our best."

Gavinaugh looked on Kifus with compassion. "Lord Kifus, I am humbled by your words, and with them I present my answer to you. The same heart beats within my chest, and the same mind orders my thoughts. The man of honor, integrity, and loyalty that stood before you then stands before you now in all completeness of mind and soul. I know that you believe this to be true of me still or you would not have ordered my chains removed just now, knowing that I have the power to kill you. You know that all of my character is intact, or I would not be standing before you. Therefore consider this, Kifus. If one of your best has not diminished in any way that makes a man a Noble Knight, then the cause to which he now has dedicated his life cannot be the fabric of foolishness or deception, but simply the truth."

Gavinaugh let his reply marinate in the logical mind of Kifus for a few moments. Kifus appeared to consider his words carefully.

"Lord Kifus, I do not lie, and yet I tell you that I have seen a dead man appear to me and tell me that He is the King's Son. You have called me one of the best, and yet I stand before you to tell you that I am the least worthy of all, for I know and have seen the perfection of the Prince. The man we killed is indeed the Son of the King, and yet He is willing to forgive all if only we believe in Him and follow Him. Consider this with all gravity—if what I have said is deceit, then nothing for you changes, and I will have wasted my life in the pursuit of folly. But if what I have said is true, then you are hanging by the thread of a web above the fires of Sedah."

Kifus's eyes slowly widened and his face became as a dying man, full of fear. He went to a chair and sat heavily upon it, and it seemed as if his legs had lost their strength. He was silent for a moment and then appeared to recover himself slightly.

Kifus looked up at Gavinaugh. "Almost…almost you convince me, Gavin." He then stood up. "Guard!"

The guard entered the room, and Kifus turned his back to Gavinaugh.

"Take him back to his cell."

Two days later, Kifus called Gavinaugh into the Great Hall before the assembly of the Noble Knights, and there was much discussion as to what should be done with him.

"He is a traitor, and traitors deserve death!" Jayden said, and many agreed.

"He was a Noble Knight," another knight said. "We would disgrace ourselves by killing one of our own, no matter what his crime."

There was great division among them, and Kifus was clearly at odds about what to do. Sir Camden rose to speak.

"Lord Kifus…Gavin is truly an enemy of our great city, but let us not forget the lesson we so painfully learned in our handling of the stranger. By our execution of Him, we created a martyr, and His treachery now has born a life of its own that we cannot seem to kill. Let us not foolishly do the same with this man."

Camden allowed the knights time to reflect on his words. "I suggest we make Sir Gavin disappear quietly," he said finally and then sat down.

Kifus rose and approached Gavinaugh.

"Sir Camden, you have spoken wisely. The last thing we want is for this traitor to become famous in his death."

He walked a circle around Gavinaugh and stopped before him.

"I have an association with the Namorians that should serve us well in regard to this criminal." Kifus looked into Gavinaugh's eyes briefly and then turned away. "Put him back in prison until Captain Dante arrives from Namor," he commanded, then exited the Great Hall.

Gavinaugh was five days in the prison cell with only water to drink and dry bread to eat. One evening, the chamber door opened and the guard escorted Leisel and another whose head was covered by a hooded cloak that hid the person's body and face.

"You may leave us," Leisel said to the guard.

"But my lady, I have been given orders by Kifus not to allow him any visitors. I am already jeopardizing…" The guard became silent as Leisel glared at him.

"As you wish, my lady." He bowed and exited.

Leisel and her companion were still at the far end of the aisle that led to the cells, where Gavinaugh was held. She turned and spoke quietly. Her companion stayed behind, and Leisel came to Gavinaugh. He was surprised, for he had not thought that he would ever see her again. They looked at each other through the iron bars and were silent for a moment.

"It is a pleasure to see you again, Leisel."

She allowed herself to smile briefly.

"I have found her," she said. "Or rather, she has found me."

Gavinaugh tilted his head slightly at her comment.

Leisel lowered her voice to almost a whisper. "She is simple…but very pretty. I can see why you are taken with her." She lowered her eyes.

Gavinaugh could not imagine what Leisel's intentions were, but he became apprehensive as he considered the possibilities.

"What is this about, Leisel? What have you done?"

Leisel looked up into his eyes, and he saw the pain of unrequited love in her countenance.

"I am not a spiteful woman, Gavin. And although her heart could never long for you as mine does, I cannot change the cruel ways of love. I do this not for her, but for you." She stepped back and looked away. A single tear trickled down her cheek, which she quickly wiped away.

"Come," she said loud enough for her companion to hear.

The hooded form came to Gavinaugh's cell and waited for Leisel to step down the aisle before removing the hood.

"Keanna!" Gavinaugh whispered.

She smiled but her eyes conveyed the ache within her soul. "Are you all right?"

Gavinaugh sensed a compassion from her that warmed his heart.

She stepped closer to the cell door, and he cursed the bars of iron between them, for he wanted to hold her. "I am, but what are you doing here? This is very dangerous. Has she threatened you?" Gavinaugh looked toward Leisel.

"No. She's been very kind. I went to her."

"But why?" he asked.

She put her hands on the bars, and he covered them with his own. She looked into his eyes. "Because I…a warrior came to me last night."

"Who was he?"

"I don't know, but he gave me a message for you. He said to tell you to be strong. You will encounter many difficulties, but the Prince will be with you. The Duke of Namor must hear your words." Keanna searched Gavinaugh's eyes. "I fear for you."

"I will be all right, Keanna."

She reached into her cloak and handed a vial to him. "He said that you must drink this."

"What is it?"

"I don't know. He said it will…protect you."

Gavinaugh removed the cork and smelled its contents. It was sweet. He lifted it to his lips, but Keanna grabbed his arm.

"What if it's poison?" she asked.

"Did you believe him?"

Keanna thought for a moment and slowly nodded her head.

"That is all I need," he said and swallowed the liquid. Its taste belied its aroma, for it was very bitter.

"Are Weston and his family all right?" he asked.

"Yes. They are safe."

Gavinaugh felt great relief. Knowing that he had nearly caused their deaths had been a great burden to him.

"I have Triumph. He is quite agitated. I think he actually misses you," she said and tried to smile.

"We must go," Leisel called to Keanna.

Keanna leaned closer to the bars, and Gavinaugh touched her face tenderly. "I will come back to you," he said.

She reached up and brushed his hand with her own and then covered her head with the hood. She walked over to Leisel, and they turned to ascend the stairs.

"Leisel!" Gavinaugh called.

She stopped and turned back to look at him.

"Thank you."

She gave a slight nod and left.

The following morning, Gavinaugh was taken to the docks, where a large three-masted ship with a foreign flag was waiting. On the deck of the ship, a prominent-looking fellow greeted Kifus and his knights with a broad grin.

"Welcome aboard the *Raven,* Lord Kifus."

"Captain Dante, it is a pleasure to see you again."

The men shook hands, and the captain looked closely at Gavinaugh. "I must say that your prisoner does not have the look of a criminal about him."

"Do not be deceived, Captain," Kifus said. "This man is as dangerous as they come. If I were you, I would leave the fetters securely upon his limbs throughout the journey."

Dante scrutinized Gavinaugh. "His sword?"

Kifus handed Gavinaugh's sword to the captain, and he fastened it about his own waist.

"My first mate has informed me that your payment has been received, and now we have your prisoner. On my honor I swear to deliver him to Duke Vespas in Namor. And now we must be off before the seas turn against us," he said.

Kifus and his men left the ship, and Gavinaugh was taken to a lower deck, where he was locked inside a small, bare room. Soon the crew was occupied with getting the vessel underway.

Gavinaugh was not given any food or water the entire day. He became queasy but was not sure if it was from the rolling of the ship, lack of food, or both. In his solitude and distress, he thought of Keanna, and the image of her in his mind brought great comfort. In the bowels of a foreign vessel en route to unknown perils, Gavinaugh resolved to take deliberate action to win her heart if he should survive this trek and see her again.

The day wore on, and toward what he thought must be evening, the door opened and a seaman took Gavinaugh to the captain's quarters.

The captain dismissed the seaman and turned to Gavinaugh. Captain Dante was a fair bit older than Gavinaugh, but age had not diminished his strength or stature. He was a tall man with a stark white beard that matched his hair. Perhaps forty years old, his hair had turned color early, and it gave him a distinctive look for his age.

Gavinaugh saw a table full of food in the center of the room. The pangs of hunger tore at him, and he was feeling faint. He found it difficult to stand, but he remained still.

"So you are the man who has caused such turmoil in Chessington— and in the entire kingdom, I am told." He smiled crookedly. "What have you done to cause Kifus to hire my ship and exile you to Namor? And why doesn't he just kill you?"

He did not wait for an answer, but turned away and walked to a cabinet nearby.

"Lord Kifus says you are a dangerous man, but my men have told me stories that say otherwise. Are you a dangerous man, Sir Gavin, or is it Gavinaugh?" This time he stared at Gavinaugh and expected an answer.

"My name is Gavinaugh, Captain. I serve the King of Arrethtrae and His Son, the Prince. Only men who are afraid of the truth are threatened by me," Gavinaugh replied.

"And what is this truth?" Dante asked.

"That the Prince is the Son of the King, who came to deliver us from the bondage of the Dark Knight and his evil work. And that by believing in Him, we are set free."

The captain stared silently at Gavinaugh, then suddenly burst into laughter. "And this is what Kifus is afraid of?" He laughed all the harder.

He removed a set of keys from the cabinet and began to unlock the fetters that were latched upon Gavinaugh's wrists and ankles. As they fell from his limbs, the captain reached for Gavinaugh's sword, which he had secured about himself, and became very serious.

"If you should try to escape or bring any treachery to my ship, I will slit your throat with your own sword. I wear the blade of my prisoner until he is delivered as a reminder of my blood-sworn duty. Will you comply, Gavinaugh?"

"I will, Captain. I swear it."

"I believe you, for though you are an enemy of Kifus, I think you are also a man of honor. Come sit with me and eat. I desire to hear more of your strange and 'frightful' words," he said as he seated Gavinaugh at his table.

Gavinaugh thought he had never tasted anything better than the food he ate at that meal. Their conversation focused on the Prince, and the captain listened intently to all he had to say.

"You are an odd fellow, Gavinaugh," he said at the end of the meal. "And your words are strange indeed. A bit too strange for my liking, but I do not see the danger in them as Kifus does."

Gavinaugh thanked the captain for the delicious food, and from that day forward he had freedom to roam the ship at will. They journeyed southeast into the seas of the Namorian realm, and Gavinaugh wondered about his future. One evening, after many days of voyage, Gavinaugh could see dark clouds in the distance that met the watery horizon, but he looked beyond them to the brilliance of an enlightened kingdom—a kingdom under the wise rule of the Prince.

CHAPTER TWELVE

TEMPESTS!

 The weather was fair, but the winds were not favorable for their trek. Captain Dante was not pleased with their progress. After two weeks at sea, the *Raven* and her crew were only little more than halfway to the ports of Namor. Gavinaugh and Captain Dante engaged themselves in lengthy discussions regarding the Prince and the future of Arrethtrae. Although Dante was intrigued by the bizarre story of a man who had risen from death to return one day to rule the kingdom, he was certainly far from becoming a Follower. Occasionally he reminded Gavinaugh sternly, usually in the presence of his crew, that he was a prisoner destined to spend the rest of his life in the dungeons of Namor. In the solitude of their evening discussions, however, Gavinaugh sensed that Dante looked fondly upon his prisoner.

Captain Dante's first mate was a gruff character named Huntly. The man had little time for silly discussions of affairs that had nothing to do with sailing the *Raven*. He was the perfect man for his position, for the crew both feared and respected him. He was the fierce disciplinarian of the command duo, which allowed the captain to appear more conciliatory toward the men without appearing weak. Gavinaugh noted that this gave the captain an effective tool to hold in reserve for times of retribution or adversity. His demeanor was seldom unpleasant, so when he became grave in his speech or bearing, the men took his commands as though their lives depended on it…and often this was true. Such was the case on a blisteringly hot afternoon when the lookout shouted a warning cry from the crow's nest that sent chills up the spines of all the crew.

"Tempests!" the man shouted and pointed off the starboard.

In that single warning, the tension onboard escalated to a state that amazed Gavinaugh. All hands instantly became still, and the focus of the entire crew went to the direction indicated by the lookout. Gavinaugh joined Captain Dante and First Mate Huntly at the starboard rail and scanned the horizon.

"How many?" Huntly shouted up to the lookout.

"Three…at least!"

"Do you think they've made us, Cap'n?" Huntly asked.

"We wouldn't be seeing them if they hadn't first seen us," Dante said with great concern on his face.

"What are Tempests?" Gavinaugh asked.

"They're the piranhas of the open seas." Dante didn't take his eyes from the black specks on the horizon. "Their ships are light and fast. They sail in fleets to overwhelm the ships they attack. Every man aboard will wish he was in the dungeons of Namor rather than to fall prey to the likes of these barbarians."

Dante turned to Huntly. "Set sail with the winds, no matter the direction. Lighten the ship and make for speed, Huntly!"

"Aye, aye, sir!" Huntly began barking orders to the men. It took no small effort to break them from their fearful trance, but once the reality of the situation sank in, their fervor in their duties was apparent.

As the afternoon passed, the specks on the horizon became the distinct forms of sailing vessels, and there was no doubt as to their course. The lookout in the crow's nest had been replaced and appeared nearly overcome with apprehension as he stepped onto the ship's deck.

"Anything else to report, Denton?" Dante asked.

"I saw at least six ships, and they're gaining on us fast! What are we going to do, Cap'n?" The man's fear was rising with each word he spoke.

"Be at ease, seaman," Dante said.

"Is it true about what they do to their captives?" Denton asked.

"Report to Huntly," the captain said without responding to his question.

The man lowered his eyes. "Aye, aye, sir."

Gavinaugh waited for the man to leave. "Where do they come from?" he asked Dante.

"No one knows for sure. The myth is that they rise up out of the sea like monsters from the deep. I have never encountered the Tempests before, but I've seen the remains of those who have." Dante nearly shuddered. "The Tempests are less than human, Gavinaugh. My men would rather drown in the depths of the sea than fall into their hands."

As evening approached, the black flags of the pursuing Tempest ships were unmistakable. The captain called the first mate and two other men into his cabin to discuss their fate. Gavinaugh was allowed to stand by and listen.

"I can hardly contain the men, Cap'n," Huntly said.

"Keep them focused on their duties," Dante said. "How long before the Tempests overtake us?"

"Late afternoon tomorrow, if the winds stay as they are."

The captain focused his attention on the map before them. "Our course takes us near the Isles of Melogne. It is our only hope."

The men stared at the captain in disbelief.

"Captain, navigating through the Isles of Melogne is suicide," Huntly said. "Not to mention that the islands themselves are haunted. No man who has set foot on the islands has ever returned."

"Huntly's right, Captain," one of the other men said. "I was a shipmate onboard the *Charlotte Louise*. When we went to rescue the shipwreck of the *Peconic,* not a soul was found."

The captain looked solemnly at each of the men. "There are six Tempest ships on our heels, men. If they should catch and board us…well, I'll take my chances on the Isles of Melogne. As far as navigating through the waters, we've got the best crew in Namor. And as for the islands, I'll believe your stories of ghosts when I see them. We'll just have to keep a steady eye, a firm hand, and a stout heart. Set course for the islands, Huntly. Cast off whatever you need to in order to make the isles before the Tempests overtake us. Dismissed!"

"Aye, aye, sir," the three men said in unison as they departed.

That evening, Gavinaugh heard the splash of wares being tossed overboard as the men attempted to lighten the ship's load. By morning, however, the Tempests' ships were ominously close. One ship had outdistanced the others and was nearly upon them. The Isles of Melogne were visible ahead, but the distance was too far and the time was too short. The crew began casting everything that was not absolutely necessary overboard, but the lead Tempest ship continued to gain on them. By noon, the two ships were nearly side by side, and the grisly flag of the sinister Tempest ship matched its dark crew. Over sixty vicious seamen stood in silence with swords drawn as their shipmates brought the vessel abreast of the *Raven*. The silence of their pursuit was eerie, and the crew of the *Raven* readied themselves for the fight of their lives. If by some miracle they survived the attack of this vessel, there would still be five more to come.

Dante approached Gavinaugh. "I understand you handle a sword well."

"I can hold my own," Gavinaugh replied.

"Never before have I released a prisoner's sword to him, even when I thought I might die. But you are different, Gavinaugh." Dante loosened the scabbard and sword from about his waist and gave Gavinaugh his sword. "My death could mean your freedom."

"My freedom is not worth the death of a good man," Gavinaugh said as he secured the sword about his waist. It made him feel complete.

Dante gave a slight smile and turned his attention to the impending fight.

The two vessels were now side by side. The Tempests cast a half dozen binding ropes with hooks across the remaining distance and bound the vessels together. In an instant, the crews of the ships were entwined in a ferocious battle of flashing swords. The Tempests were merciless in their cause, and the crew of the *Raven* fought desperately against the evil sea warriors.

Gavinaugh fought gallantly and saved the lives of many men during the battle. He tried to stay close to Captain Dante, for he knew that the survival of the crew depended on this man's leadership. As the fighting progressed, Gavinaugh felt the power of the sword of the Prince pulsing through him. He sensed the tides of battle and dominated with each blow he struck.

Dante was embroiled in a desperate fight with a large Tempest who seemed impossible to defeat. Gavinaugh deflected the blade of an adversary just as the captain narrowly dodged the thrust of his grisly opponent. Gavinaugh brought a deadly slice across the torso of his enemy and then went to give aid to Dante. By the time he reached the captain, Dante had ducked beneath a high slice and executed a deadly thrust to end the life of the massive Tempest. Just then a spear flew from the Tempest ship directly at Captain Dante.

"Captain!" Huntly shouted, but the warning was too late.

The speed of the spear was great, but Gavinaugh had already initiated a response. He took one more step and timed an incredibly powerful slice downward to meet the spear as it passed by him on its path to Dante's chest. Gavinaugh's blade severed the shaft of the spear and deflected the tip so that it embedded into the main mast beside Dante.

Gavinaugh's influence in the battle was significant, for his skill and courage rallied the men to overcome in the fight against the Tempests. As the fighting lessened, Gavinaugh maneuvered his way along the starboard rail and cut the binding ropes that held the *Raven* to the Tempest ship. The ships broke apart, and the remaining Tempests onboard were quickly eliminated and cast overboard. A cheer rose up from the crew of the *Raven* because of their victory, and Gavinaugh was heralded as a hero of the battle.

Captain Dante approached Gavinaugh and thanked him for saving his life. "Why don't you hang on to that sword for a bit…just in case," Dante said as he slapped Gavinaugh on the back.

The fanfare was brief, however, for the battle had significantly slowed them, and the other five vessels were closing fast. They recovered their speed and raced on toward the Isles of Melogne.

By midafternoon, the Isles of Melogne loomed large before them, and it looked as though they might make them before they were overtaken. There were five islands, all very close to each other. The main island was large with steep, rocky cliffs that comprised the northern shoreline. One of the smaller islands sat just a few hundred feet off the north shore of the main island, and the two steep cliffs on the islands formed a water canal between them.

As their ship approached, large rock outcroppings began to appear above and below the waterline.

"Captain, we will tear the hull apart if we hit these rocks," Huntly said.

Death pursued them from behind, and calamity awaited them ahead. It was a precarious situation, and Gavinaugh could feel the crew's apprehension.

"Slow our speed and mark the depth," Dante ordered. "There must be a canal deep enough. The cliffs of those islands surely go deeper than the waterline. Make our way for the canal."

Although the Tempest ships continued to gain, it was apparent that they too had slowed their approach in the treacherous waters of the isles.

The crew worked intently, and everyone held their breath at one point as the hull scraped along the jagged edge of an unseen rock formation. As they navigated their way to the channel between the two islands, the Tempest vessels stopped their pursuit, but did not retreat. The ships formed a barricade between the open sea and the channel of the two islands, thereby trapping the *Raven* within the confines of the islands. They were now at the mercy of the legends of the Isles of Melogne. Most of their supplies had been cast off and their route blocked, but they were alive. They turned their attention from the perils of the sea to the challenges of survival in a haunted land. 🔲

CHAPTER THIRTEEN

THE ISLES OF MELOGNE

The canal narrowed even further the deeper they progressed, and the cliffs of the two shores beside them rose high above. The islands were dense with trees and vegetation. The men occasionally heard the sound of an animal that was unknown to them, and it brought chills. Fortunately, Dante was correct and the canal was deep enough for the *Raven* to continue onward. Halfway through the canal, the cliffs dropped quickly to meet a grassy shoreline. The canal widened for a short distance and formed an alcove. The captain ordered the crew to set anchor. The serene landscape engulfed the ship in wild beauty.

They did not know how long the Tempests would wait for them, but Dante reckoned that they would exhaust their food and water long before the Tempests gave up. He formed a landing party of fifteen men to see what was available on the island, but those he selected were not pleased. Huntly remained on the *Raven* while Gavinaugh and Captain Dante went with the men to shore.

As the crew pulled their boat ashore, they determined a direction to begin their search and proceeded inland a fair distance before stopping to rest. They found a clearing and set up a base camp to facilitate further searches into the island.

After a short time, one of the men came running to the captain.

"Captain! Look!"

The man pointed into the trees beyond the clearing, and Gavinaugh saw what was causing his concern. Amidst the trees, thirty to forty figures stood with spears in their hands. Gavinaugh wondered if this was perhaps the source of the legends of the ghosts on the islands.

The men all rose and drew their swords, but the shadowy figures remained still. Eventually, Dante and Gavinaugh sheathed their swords and slowly approached the native islanders with open arms. Dante and Gavinaugh stopped midway, and one of them walked toward Dante. His hair was long and tied back at his neck. His skin was slightly darker than theirs, but there was little difference in the features of his face. He wore crude clothing made of leather.

The man came within two steps of Dante and Gavinaugh and stopped. He stared intently as if he had never seen the likes of such men before.

"We are in search of food and water. Can you help us?" Dante asked.

Gavinaugh wondered if the man could even understand them. Then the man spoke.

"Yes, we can help you. Where are you from?" The man's accent was strange, but he spoke with a clarity that surprised both of them.

"I am Dante. I come from Namor. This is Gavinaugh. He comes from Chessington."

The man thought for a moment. "I have heard of such places. My name is Pliubus, chief of the Melitans. These are my people," he said, motioning toward the trees. Those with him came out of the trees and stood in the open.

"You are fleeing the Tempests," the chief said.

"Yes. How did you know?" Dante asked.

"We are always aware of the Tempests when they are near. They will not attack you on the island," he said.

Pliubus and his people went to the camp with the men. As they entered, the chief became concerned and lifted his spear. His men did the same, and Dante's men drew their swords.

"You should not be here!" Pliubus said sternly. He did not appear concerned with Dante's men but instead looked to the trees.

Captain Dante tried to calm the situation. "What is wrong, Pliubus?"

Pliubus and his men be-
gan to step back to where
they had come from. "It is
the strangler vine...you must
leave!"

Suddenly, the man next
to Gavinaugh screamed and
fell to the ground. He clawed
at the dirt, but something
unseen was dragging him
toward a large tree at the
edge of their camp.

"It is too late!" screamed
Pliubus. His men shouted in
fear and backed farther away, searching the ground as they went.

The seaman continued to scream, and Gavinaugh dove for him. He locked hands, but whatever was pulling the man was overpowering both of them.

"My leg...my leg!" the man screamed, and Gavinaugh could see that a vine as thick as a man's thumb had wrapped completely around his lower leg.

Gavinaugh stood, drew his sword, and ran ahead of the man. The vine was buried in the vegetation of the forest floor, but he could see its movement beneath the leaves. He made a quick slice and severed the vine. Then he helped the man to his feet, and they ran away from the large tree. Three paces later, Gavinaugh felt a pull on his own leg, and before he could react he was prone on the ground and being yanked back toward the tree. A vine had wrapped around his leg, and another was encircling his waist. Its squeeze was powerful. Dante drew his sword and began to run toward Gavinaugh, but the chief stopped him.

"It's too late, you cannot stop it!" he exclaimed. "You will die too!"

As the chief spoke the words, the entire ground for twenty paces around the tree came to life as dozens of vines surfaced from beneath the overlying leaves and grass. The trunk of the huge tree also seemed to move as vertical strips of thick bark separated from the base of the tree but remained connected farther up the trunk. Each moving piece served as an arm with bonelike spikes that swung outward to strike the flesh of any prey captured by the vines. Little did Gavinaugh know that the poisoned spikes on the limbs paralyzed their prey until the juices of the vine could digest it. Like some enormous woody octopus, the tree was a frightening oracle of horror.

Gavinaugh felt the grip of the vine tightening about his leg and waist and the air being forced from his lungs. He saw dozens of vines surface around him and knew that he had only a moment to react. Thankfully his left arm was still free. The vines had dragged him about six paces from the tree, nearly within reach of the spiked arms from the trunk that were flailing through the air around its base.

Gavinaugh made a quick slice across the vine that encircled his waist and then another across the vine about his leg. He tried to stand, but another wrapped around his right arm and pulled him to the ground. He cut it and quickly stood up. He knew it was paramount that his sword arm remain free. Everywhere he looked, vines were whipping about him and closing in. *Whoosh!* One of the trunk arms flew past his chest, just missing its mark.

Knowing there was no escape, Gavinaugh did not run. He focused his mind as though he were facing the blades of a dozen

Shadow Warriors and began to cut and slice each vine that came within reach of his sword. With the training of the Prince, he could almost see the vines behind him as they prepared to strike. One vine reached from below and grabbed his leg. He bent slightly to sever it and felt a strong, painful blow from one of the trunk arms. In his fight with the vines, he had stepped too close to the tree, and the spikes from one of the arms had pierced his back. Gavinaugh tried to ignore the pain and swung powerfully at the arm as it poised for another strike. His sword cut clean through the arm and left a weapon-less limb flailing in the air. Then Gavinaugh methodically worked his way about the tree, severing each limb and vine that appeared until all about him was still.

Gavinaugh backed away from the tree until he was at a safe distance. Only then did he allow himself to relax. The pain in his back returned, but it wasn't as severe as when he was first struck.

Dante, Pliubus, and all of their men ran to him and looked at him in awe. Pliubus examined the wound in his back and noticed that it was already beginning to heal. He knelt before Gavinaugh.

"No man has ever survived the grip of the strangler vine. You are a supreme knight!" he said, kneeling and bowing his head. All of his men did the same.

Gavinaugh reached for the man's shoulder. "No, Pliubus, I am not a supreme knight, but I will tell you of One who is. It is His sword, His training, and His power that have allowed me to survive. Rise up."

Pliubus took Gavinaugh, Dante, and his men into their village that day and gave them shelter and food. The group stayed for three days, gathering food and water for their ship. Pliubus and his people showed great kindness to the men and taught them how to identify the trees infected with the strangler vines. During this time, Pliubus and his people listened earnestly as Gavinaugh told them about the Prince.

During an afternoon meal, one of the villagers urgently approached Pliubus. "Chief Pliubus, your father has been taken!"

Pliubus rose up from the table. "What?"

"Your father and three others have been taken by Lord Malthos. A terrible fate has fallen upon our village!" he declared.

Pliubus sank to his seat in a daze and did not rush out at the news, as Gavinaugh expected.

"Pliubus, there are many of us. We will help you recover your father…from whoever has taken him," Gavinaugh said as he rose from the table.

Pliubus looked blankly at Gavinaugh. "There is no hope. The one who has taken him is much too powerful." He put his head in his hands.

"Who is this man, and where is he?" Dante asked.

Pliubus looked up and seemed hesitant to answer. "Toward the center of the island, in the Valley of Shadows, there is a castle. He who lives there has dominion over this island. I am sorry…I should have told you earlier…but it was so good to see people from other lands, and I did not want to frighten you off." Pliubus said and lowered his eyes.

"What should you have told us?" Dante asked, quite concerned.

"You have heard, no doubt, that the Isles of Melogne are haunted."

Dante nodded. "Yes, but we thought perhaps it was because of the Tempests or the strangler vines."

"No, it is because of Lord Malthos. Anyone who comes to the island never leaves. He is lord over this island. Our village exists to serve him. He will never let us leave." Pliubus became sober. "You will either serve him or die, but you will never leave. It is my fault… I should have warned you at the very first. But when we saw the power of Sir Gavinaugh over the strangler vine…I had to know more." The man lowered his eyes and stared at the table.

Gavinaugh reached across and grabbed Pliubus's arm. "It's all right, Pliubus. Your warning would not have changed anything."

Pliubus looked up. "He is punishing me for showing you kindness.

That's why he has taken my father and the others. Each winter we are required to send two servants to his castle to be his slaves. No one ever comes back. It is not yet time, but he has taken four. You should leave quickly…if you can."

"But he is just one man," Dante said. "How can he stop a ship full of mighty men from leaving?"

Pliubus shook his head. "He is not just one man…he is like many men, and his power is great. I've seen him destroy ten men at once as if they were but children. You and your ship are in grave danger. It may be too late already." His voice was devoid of expression.

Dante rose up. "My ship! We must leave at once!"

"Captain Dante, I know of this Malthos," Gavinaugh said. "He is an enemy of the Prince. See about your men, but I want Pliubus to take me to his castle."

"No!" cried Pliubus. "I will be killed, and so will you!"

Gavinaugh looked straight at him. "Your father may still be alive."

Pliubus sat back in his chair and his shoulders fell. "I will take you," he said softly.

"Are you sure you want to do this?" Dante asked Gavinaugh.

"I am called to it."

"Very well. One of my men will accompany you. I will wait to hear from him what has become of you." Dante exited quickly and assigned a man to go with Gavinaugh and Pliubus.

Gavinaugh, Pliubus, and the shipmate journeyed farther into the island until they came to the Valley of Shadows, which was surrounded by hills that rose high above them. Deep in the valley stood a massive dark castle. Pliubus became stricken with fear—so much so that Gavinaugh had to encourage him to continue. As they descended into the trees of the valley, Gavinaugh could feel the oppression all around him. He reached for the hilt of his sword, and it brought him great comfort.

"We are close," Pliubus whispered.

They proceeded cautiously and then stopped at the edge of the forest, which gave way to the castle grounds. The towers of the great castle loomed large, and the walls looked massive.

Gavinaugh started toward the castle.

Pliubus grabbed his arm. "He will kill you, Gavinaugh." His eyes were wide, and his hand was shaking.

Gavinaugh looked at him and smiled. "The Prince is greater than any dark warrior," Gavinaugh said as he drew his sword. "*He* is the sword."

Gavinaugh held the brilliant silver sword before him, and it seemed to reverberate within his grip. He walked into the open and up to the massive gates, leaving Pliubus and his escort in the cover of the trees.

"Malthos!" he shouted. "Release your slaves!"

A moment of silence followed, and then the gates of the castle began to open. Deep, ugly laughter echoed out into the forest from behind the doors. The opening widened until the monstrous form of a dark warrior appeared. He drew his sword and came toward Gavinaugh.

The laughter turned to loathing. "Who dares enter my domain?" With each step, the form of the warrior grew, until he stood but a few paces away, towering over Gavinaugh like the castle behind him. His hair was black and hung to his shoulders. His face bore the deep scar of his master and revealed the utter hatred that emanated from his soul. He flexed the large muscles in his chest and arms, which seemed to expand his size. He was not a man—he was a giant. The sword he wielded was a picture of evil. The blade was long and contained engravings that were dark and unidentifiable. The hilt had short, wicked bladelike protrusions similar to the ones that had impaled Gavinaugh many years earlier in the forest on the road to Denrith.

Gavinaugh stayed silent as he beheld the warrior. He felt the apprehension rising within him until he remembered the Prince.

"I will cut out your heart and feed it to my dogs, fool!" the beast of a man said with disgust. He began to draw back his sword.

"I am Gavinaugh, servant of the Prince!"

The warrior hesitated, and Gavinaugh saw a fleeting glimpse of concern cross his face at the mention of the Prince.

"Your dominion over these people will come to an end, for by the power of the Prince and by His name I command you to release your captives!" Gavinaugh spoke the words with great authority.

Malthos seemed paralyzed. It was a strange picture to behold, for the simple and powerful words of a faithful servant of the Prince had caused the heart of a monster to tremble.

The warrior shook himself and roared in defiance. He attacked Gavinaugh ferociously. Gavinaugh defended himself against the beast's massive blows. The strength of his sword matched the image of his power, and Gavinaugh found himself retreating against the onslaught. Yet he also felt the strength of the Prince rising within him as he bore the fury of the warrior. The grisly sword came streaking toward Gavinaugh, and he brought an upward deflecting blow to meet it. As he did so, he ducked beneath the colliding blades and executed a counter slice that tore through Malthos's left side. The warrior screamed in agony.

Malthos stepped back and looked at Gavinaugh incredulously. His disbelief turned quickly to fierce anger, and he came at Gavinaugh with more fury than before. His sword came perilously close to Gavinaugh's neck, but Gavinaugh did not retreat this time. He stood his ground and the fight raged on. Gavinaugh was tiring, but the warrior was growing weak from his wound as well. In one quick and explosive maneuver, Gavinaugh deflected and thrust so quickly that the warrior could not recover. His blade pierced Malthos's chest. He dropped to his knees as his dark weapon loosened from his grip and fell harmlessly to the ground.

"The power of the Prince overcomes all evil—even that of the Dark Knight and his Shadow Warriors!" Gavinaugh proclaimed.

"No!" Malthos gasped with his last breath. He collapsed to the ground and died.

Pliubus and the escort slowly crept toward Gavinaugh with their eyes fixed on the hulking mass that lay at his feet. They looked as though he might rise up and slay them at any moment, but their fear was for naught.

They walked through the gates of the castle and entered a world of despair and death. They opened the cells and released all those Malthos had held captive. Pliubus found his father, and their reunion was joyful. Many villagers of years past were freed that day, and Pliubus wept for the freedom that Gavinaugh had brought his people by the sword of the Prince.

Gavinaugh embraced his new friend and then departed later that day with his escort to join Dante and the rest of the crew of the *Raven*. The escort described to Captain Dante all that had happened, and he marveled at Gavinaugh's skill. Dante allowed Gavinaugh to retain his sword, for he had proven his word and his integrity to the captain. Never before had Dante encountered such a man as Gavinaugh, and he came to realize that the man's call to the Prince bound his heart more than any fetters of iron ever could.

There was no sign of the Tempests on their departure, and their journey to Namor continued uneventfully. Upon their arrival, Captain Dante vouched for Gavinaugh and was given charge over him. Dante brought him into his home and allowed him great freedom until the time that he should appear before the Duke of Namor. During that time, Gavinaugh formed a new haven of Followers, for many longed to hear the words of the Prince and the hope that He brought. Through it all, Gavinaugh and Dante became close friends.

On the appointed day, Gavinaugh stood before the Duke of Namor and declared the Prince before him and before the council that had been convened to hear his testimony. Because of the duke's association with Lord Kifus, Gavinaugh was not set free, but it was declared that he should remain under Dante's custody. Dante granted all freedom to Gavinaugh—with the exception of traveling to Chessington, since such an act would cause severe turmoil between the two great cities and their leaders.

Gavinaugh missed his friends, especially Keanna, for his mind had never wandered far from the affectionate thoughts he had for her. One morning, Dante called Gavinaugh to the parlor of his estate. As Gavinaugh entered the parlor, great joy filled his heart, for Weston, Sandon, and Keanna stood before him with smiles that reflected his own delight.

"My dear friends!" he exclaimed and embraced Weston and Sandon.

"Gavinaugh, you look well!" Weston said, smiling.

"And you."

He turned to Keanna and drank in the smile on her lips. He embraced her as one would a friend, but his heart embraced her as much more. His stomach flipped within him at her touch.

"It is good to see you," he said and stepped back to look at them all. "I never expected to see you in Namor."

"Captain Dante sent for us when you arrived. It's taken us many days to reach you," Sandon said. "As usual, we hear you have already caused quite a stir in the city."

Gavinaugh smiled. "There are Knights of the Prince everywhere… they just don't know it yet."

"We brought Triumph with us," Keanna said.

"Did he miss me too?"

"Who said we missed you?" Sandon quipped. "We're here to try and keep you under control this time," he said, and they all laughed heartily.

Dante invited the friends to remain at his estate as long as they desired, and they used the time to build up the Knights of the Prince in Namor. Their work made knights of many people, and eventually there was no small stirring among the leadership.

Gavinaugh, Weston, Sandon, and Keanna departed Namor to seek the hearts of others for the Prince. They journeyed north along the base of the Boundary Mountains. With each day that passed, Gavinaugh came to long for the time when he would see the Prince again. It was a hope that propelled him forward and brought passion to his work.

CHAPTER FOURTEEN

A PRINCESS
YET TO BE

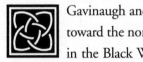Gavinaugh and his comrades traveled along the mountains toward the northern country, making camp in the evenings in the Black Woods. Gavinaugh was grateful for the companionship of his friends. They were true friends who had endured much with him and because of him. Weston had sacrificed his life of comfort and his family's security because of his love for the Prince. Sandon had abandoned all for the same. Gavinaugh's zeal to fulfill the mission given him by the Prince had brought great adversity and at times heartache to them and those they loved.

Keanna, however, had chosen to stay by his side for reasons he had yet to fully discover. He knew that at first it was because she wanted to kill him. Then he believed it was because she had nowhere to go. But now he was not sure.

It was almost too hard to have her near now, for he had come to love her so deeply that he was continually preoccupied with thoughts of her. He'd never really had the opportunity to tell her about his feelings, or at least that was what he told himself. In truth, his silence was in part because of the possibility that she might not reciprocate his love. He marveled at the difference between his courage in battle and his cowardice in love.

At Thecia he had confirmed in his heart that she was much more to him than a friend, and every day that had passed his feelings for her had grown deeper. However, there was an unresolved matter that disquieted his mind and brought war to his heart. It was why he now hesitated to discuss a relationship with her, for she had never fully expressed her belief in the Prince. It was a matter that he knew he must resolve, for the condition of his heart and the energy within his being were undeniably tied to her.

The Black Woods was a place of beauty and charm. It beckoned to the heart. One evening, Gavinaugh came to sit beside Keanna during their evening meal. The conversation between the four of them consisted of tales of past adventures and eventually turned to laughter as they recounted the incident at Penwell and the governor's response to the Silent Warriors.

Although the woods were full of shadows, the midsummer's light was far from ending. After the meal, Gavinaugh found an occasion to speak with Keanna alone.

"Keanna, would you care to take a ride with me?" he asked.

"Yes, I would enjoy that."

They mounted their steeds and left camp to explore the beauty of the woods. The forest canopy provided a cathedral of green, and the cool of the evening was a relief from the heat of the afternoon. They stopped at a small stream and knelt down to drink the cold water. Gavinaugh watched Keanna as she lifted the water to her lips with her cupped hand. He was once again mesmerized by her movements and by her form. Everything about her seemed to capture his attention. He felt alive and foolish at the same time. He understood the natural attraction of a man to a woman, but there was something so much deeper that drew him to her. When she looked at him, her eyes became a window to her soul, and he felt as though he were peering into the future of the kingdom. It was an indescribable feeling that took possession of him.

Gavinaugh stood and offered a hand to lift her from the stream's edge. She took his hand, stood, and looked at him with warm eyes. He lingered just a moment before releasing her hand.

"I have a gift for you," he said with a smile and went to retrieve a package wrapped in soft leather from Triumph's pack. He handed the package to her.

Keanna looked astonished, and hesitated in accepting it. "But I—"

"Please, Keanna," Gavinaugh interrupted.

Her eyes welled up with tears.

"You have been so kind to me," she said as she slowly took the package from him. She ran her hand over the top of the string that held the parcel tight.

After a moment, Gavinaugh could not wait any longer. "Are you going to open it?"

"Do I have to?" she asked.

"That *is* the point of the gift—to be opened," he said with a gentle laugh.

"But once I do, the unopened gift will be gone forever."

Gavinaugh gazed at the beauty of her wonder and her humility and let his heart slip a little further into her embrace.

"Take forever if you wish. Forgive me for allowing my impatience to rob you of this moment."

She smiled at him sweetly.

After another moment Keanna slowly untied the string and opened the soft leather. Her first glimpse was of a beautiful cream cloth. Her mouth parted slightly, and a sense of awe was on her face as she lifted up a simple but elegant dress, fit for a princess.

"When I saw the dress in Namor, I could not refrain from purchasing it for you," Gavinaugh said, enjoying Keanna's expression.

The tears began to flow freely as she gazed at the beauty of the dress. "Gavinaugh, I am just a peasant girl. I could never wear such a beautiful garment as this," she said as she tried to give it back to him.

"I have been in the presence of nobility all my life, Keanna, and I have yet to see a lady who compares with you. The Prince has opened my eyes to true nobility, and His kingdom belongs to hearts such as yours. Please accept it. Whether you wear the dress or not does not change the fact that you are a princess, both to the King and to me."

She held the dress close to her and then quickly hugged Gavinaugh. She backed away and blushed.

"Thank you, Gavinaugh. It is beyond beautiful, and I should never be worthy to wear it," she said.

"Nonsense! Try it and let us see if *it* is worthy of *you*!"

She looked wistfully into his eyes. "As a little girl, I always dreamed of wearing such a gown, and here it is in my hands. Dare I?"

"I insist," he said.

She smiled. "As you wish, Sir Gavinaugh."

She walked a short distance into the forest, behind a growth of thick shrubbery, while Gavinaugh turned and tended to the horses. He searched Keanna's pack on her horse and discovered the royal robe he had bequeathed her at the Tournament of Lords in Thecia. A moment later she called to him.

As Gavinaugh caught his first glimpse of Keanna, he was enamored by her beauty, for she possessed all the dignity of a lady of great stature. He stopped a few paces away and gazed upon her, entranced by the graceful lines of her form and the radiance of her face. Against the lush backdrop of the forest walls, Gavinaugh imprinted the image in his mind, hoping never to forget this moment. Keanna blushed at his gaze and looked down at the gown.

"I feel quite ridiculous. I will take it off," she said and turned away.

"No!" Gavinaugh exclaimed. "You look beautiful!"

She smiled in response.

"Something is missing," he said. He walked back to her horse and pulled out the robe from Thecia and placed it about her shoulders. He stepped back and bowed before her.

She curtsied and laughed.

"I was correct, however. The dress is not worthy of you, for its elegance has diminished in the presence of your charm," Gavinaugh said.

She shook her head and came to his side. "Shall we walk, sir?"

He smiled and offered his arm, and she took it. They walked in the beauty of the forest scenery, content to let the kingdom pass them by for a time. They came to a large fallen tree and sat upon its trunk. Gavinaugh resisted what he knew he must ask, for he didn't want the delight of this evening to end. But eventually his peace escaped him anyway, and he became quiet.

"What is bothering you?" she asked.

"May I ask a question of you?"

"Of course," she replied.

He hesitated. "I have given my life in service to the Prince because I believe in Him."

Keanna turned her eyes away from him.

"He is the reason I am alive today. He is the reason for which I live. Do you understand what this means for me?"

"Yes, I do," she replied.

"Keanna, do you believe in the Prince?"

She looked back at Gavinaugh, and he saw the conflict within her. She was silent for a time before she spoke.

"It is the Prince who has brought us together, and it is the Prince who keeps us apart, isn't it?" she said with a hint of sadness in her voice.

"It is," he said. He turned to face her and looked into her eyes as he had never dared before. "Keanna, you have so captured my heart and soul that I cannot bear to think of life without you. I dared not tell you before, for I did not know if you could ever forgive me for the agony I caused you and your family. But now I cannot bear it any longer. My heart is yours to do with as you please, but I first must know that I have given it to one who serves the Prince as I do."

She blinked and a tear fell down her cheek, but it was not shed out of delight. He could see the turmoil in Keanna's countenance and could hardly bear the possibility of what her words might reveal. He lifted his hand to her cheek and wiped away the tear, then turned aside.

"Gavinaugh, it would be a crime against our hearts to offer anything less than pure truth." She lifted her hand to his chin and turned his gaze back to her. More tears streaked her face, but Gavinaugh did not wipe them away, for each touch of her skin only melded his heart to the anchor of what seemed to be an impossible love.

"Do you love another, then?" he asked brokenheartedly.

"I have given my love to no one. When the Shadow Warriors killed my parents and sold me into slavery, I wanted to die myself. When I did not die, I wanted revenge. The Prince robbed me of my revenge, but I am grateful, for you have dared my heart to hope again." She paused and looked at the ground.

Gavinaugh felt as though he were perched at the edge of a cliff, trying to keep his balance.

"Until this moment I did not think it possible that I could win the heart of such a noble knight as you." She turned back and looked into his eyes. "But I have always known that any love in my heart I might offer you must be freed by the One you serve. I have seen how your loyalty to the Prince transcends even your own desires."

She cried softly. "I have heard your words of the Prince and yearn for them to be my own, but the pain of my past has imprisoned me. Answer me one question, Gavinaugh, that I might believe."

Gavinaugh found a sliver of hope in her words and yet became afraid. *What if I cannot answer this question? Will I doom her to destruction and to a life without love?*

"What is this question that so haunts your soul?"

She hesitated, and he ached to hold and comfort her.

"If the Prince truly cares for this kingdom, why does He allow such great pain?" She asked it with such passion that Gavinaugh felt her soul tremble.

Gavinaugh reached out and placed her delicate hand in his own.

"Oh, Keanna, the whole of my being desires to give an answer that will satisfy your soul, but I fear that you will find my words inadequate."

He paused to gather his thoughts. *Give me the words, my Prince, to show her the depth of Your wisdom and Your love.*

Gavinaugh looked down at Keanna's hand. "You must first understand that it is the Dark Knight who has brought such great pain to the kingdom. He has turned the hearts of the people away from the King and His goodness. The King desires all people to return to Him, but because of their pride and foolishness, many will never choose to follow Him. This pain and suffering is allowed for a time to reveal the treachery of Lucius. But do not think the King unmerciful or unfeeling, for He sent His one and only Son to endure more pain and suffering than any other man in the kingdom ever has, even unto death."

Gavinaugh paused to see if Keanna was accepting any of his words. Her tears had stopped, and she looked at him as though she wanted to hear more.

"But here is the beauty of the Prince, Keanna. When we serve Him wholly, He can turn all of our pain caused by Lucius's vilest intentions into a glorious victory."

"How is that possible?" she asked softly.

"There is a kingdom waiting for those who believe, where there will be no more sorrow, no more pain. If the pain we suffer brings us to that understanding and belief, then we are victorious. When the Shadow Warrior pierced me with his sword, I had an encounter with the Prince and believed. That pain bought me a place in the kingdom that is to come. Even this moment between us exists because of the pain we have suffered in our past, and I would endure the pain of a thousand swords to be in your presence this night and speak of the hope of winning your love."

Gavinaugh did not sense withdrawal in Keanna, but he wished to know her thoughts.

"A mother must labor in pain to give birth," he continued, "but in the end there is a precious new life. Our kingdom labors in pain, but in the end there is new life for those who believe. There is much pain, but the King has begun the healing through the Prince. All will suffer pain—the difference is what we choose to do with it. When we serve the Prince, our pain makes us stronger. What you have suffered, I cannot heal. But the Prince can and will."

Keanna looked at him without expression. "I must think about what you've said. Please be patient with me."

He nodded, and she stood and slowly walked away. The light of the setting sun broke through the vertical towers of the forest trees in a clearing near them, and Keanna walked toward it. Wisps of evening ground fog swirled around the beautiful gown and robe as she passed through. She was lost in heavy contemplation, and Gavinaugh hoped and waited.

The reins of his heart were pulled tight, and for the first time since he had met the Prince, his mind struggled against the desire to compromise his convictions. *What if she can't believe...does it really matter that much?* he asked himself. He rose up and lifted his eyes to the sky above and remembered his promise to the Prince to stay true to his quest: "*To the last beat of my heart, I will, my Prince...I so swear!*" He knew that his heart could not stand divided between the Prince and one who did not serve Him. He gazed at the slender form of his beautiful companion. She was standing by a large stone near the edge of the stream that watered their steeds not far away and seemed lost in the soothing sound and dancing reflections of the water.

Gavinaugh returned to recover their horses. They were grazing on the tender spires of new grass near the water's edge. Keanna was farther up the stream and just beyond his sight. He pulled on the reins and walked with the animals in that direction. After a few paces, Triumph stopped. He raised his head high and perked up his ears. Gavinaugh stroked his neck and felt the steed's powerful muscles twitch with apprehension.

"What is it, boy?"

A dreadful thought began to swell in his mind, and chills ran from his feet clear up to his neck. He had been in this arena before. Triumph looked where Keanna should be, and Gavinaugh felt the beast of fear clawing at him. All at once the forest darkened and seemed to collapse upon him. He drew his sword, but it suddenly felt as though it weighed a hundred pounds. The air about him felt as thick as syrup as he turned toward Keanna and ran that direction. The beauty of the forest devolved into limbs of evil that seemed to grasp at him as he passed by, and all his fear exploded in the sound of her scream.

"Gavinaugh!" Her voice pierced the serenity of the forest on the waves of terror.

"Keanna!" he screamed and tightened his grip on his sword. The rush within his muscles overtook the atrophy of fear, and he charged through the barriers of the forest with the power of a war-horse barreling toward its foe. The hazy picture of impending doom cleared as he drew closer, and he despaired greatly—Keanna was in the tight grip of a Shadow Warrior. Two others drew their swords and faced Gavinaugh as they heard him approach. He did not falter at the ominous image of evil in front of him as he had before. His heart was powered by the force of the Prince—and by love.

Keanna screamed again and clutched at the air between her and Gavinaugh. Panic and fear so enveloped her that he could hardly bear to see it. A vision of her face and the scene at Cartelbrook years earlier flashed across his mind. The horrific episode of their past seemed to be unfolding before his eyes once again.

CHAPTER FIFTEEN

ANCIENT ENEMIES

 Keanna's mind ran wild with fear. She could not think of any horror worse than falling once again into the steely grip of these brutish warriors. In the solace of the forest, she had come to the precipice of yielding her heart to the Prince and thus to Gavinaugh, but now her past loomed as large as a mountain, and it pressed her deep into the caverns of despair and terror. She saw Gavinaugh running toward her, but hope had already nearly abandoned her.

"You are no princess, wench." The warrior's dark voice spoke closely in her ear, and she shuddered at the sound of it. His large hand encircled her neck and squeezed so she could not scream anymore. The royal robe fell from her shoulders and was trampled beneath his boots. He handled her harshly and dragged her to his horse.

"You are a peasant and a slave, and now you will serve me in my stronghold forever!" He laughed a deep, guttural laugh that seemed to shake the forest.

She reached for Gavinaugh in desperation but was swallowed by the beast—the beast that preyed upon the blood of innocents, the beast that was never satisfied. Her will collapsed, and she became a prisoner of darkness once again.

The wicked laughter echoed through the forest and pierced Gavinaugh's heart like poisoned arrows. He reached into the depths of his soul and found the strength of a hundred men and brought it all to bear on the two warriors who stood between him and Keanna. He recognized them—these were the same ones who had come to kill him on the road to Denrith. The brute that held Keanna was the one named Devinoux.

Gavinaugh unleashed his weapon on both men with such fury that the warriors' arrogance vanished in an instant. His sword flew so swiftly that one of the warriors hesitated in amazement. Gavinaugh's blade did not tarry at the opportunity. His sword entered and exited the warrior so quickly that the brute was dead before he hit the ground. The second warrior stepped back and took a defensive posture.

Gavinaugh looked beyond him and saw the leader struggling to place Keanna on his horse. He had but a moment before he lost Keanna to the nightmare of her past. He pounced upon the second warrior with a relentless assault of cuts and slices like no man in Arrethtrae had ever endured.

"Devinoux!" the warrior shouted in a voice that manifested his fear.

Gavinaugh showed no mercy as his love was forced onto the warrior's horse. In one powerful blow, Gavinaugh's blade slammed against his foe's sword and moved it from its protective position. Gavinaugh spun and sliced through the warrior. The man fell, silenced by the sword of justice.

By now the leader had mounted, and Gavinaugh tried to reach them, but he was too late. Keanna screamed through the leader's tightened grip and fought against him, but he was too powerful to overcome. The black steed launched away from Gavinaugh, and his heart screamed in the agony of the moment.

He whistled for Triumph and heard the pounding of more horses approaching.

"Gavinaugh! What has happened?" Weston said urgently as he brought Triumph and Keanna's horse in tow. Sandon followed close behind.

"A Shadow Warrior has taken Keanna!" he said as he jumped up on Triumph.

Gavinaugh led the pursuit through the forest. He couldn't see his precious Keanna, and he urged Triumph to run faster.

"Take me to her, Triumph," he said to his faithful friend and let the animal chart the course to his love. The trees blurred past them as they pressed deeper into the forest, desperately chasing the heels of evil. The mist of the evening slowed Weston and Sandon's horses, but they continued in the reckless race with courage. Triumph seemed to know the heart of his master and the peril to his friend, for he charged forward mightily, without caution. Gavinaugh occasionally caught glimpses of the fleeing warrior and dared to let his hope return. He was gaining on them, and each stride of his powerful steed brought one more thread of hope.

Before long, he had gained enough ground to keep Keanna and the warrior in constant view, but something loomed before them like a massive dragon of the sea. As the waning light of dusk revealed the horror of the forest to Gavinaugh, his heart sank to new depths of despair. Before them stood a dozen mounted Shadow Warriors. Side by side, they formed a wall that stretched into the murky horizons of the forest vegetation. The line of warriors opened like a curtain to let the fleeing warrior and Keanna through. Then it closed back together, and Gavinaugh brought Triumph to a halt. Weston and Sandon quickly came up behind him and were speechless.

"Keanna is behind this barrier of evil, my friends. I will not abandon her to such a cruel fate, but I can't ask you to sacrifice your lives against these brutes. Leave and save yourselves," Gavinaugh said. With each passing moment, Devinoux stole Keanna farther from him, and he could hardly be still.

Weston looked at Gavinaugh. "Never abandon a fellow knight in battle or in peril," he said and drew his sword. Sandon did the same.

"The Code is not an option, Sir Gavinaugh. It is our life!" Weston lifted his sword before him.

"We outnumber them one to four," Sandon added, with a wry smile crossing his face. "What's to flee from?" He lifted his sword to join Weston's.

The three men crossed swords and shouted, "The King reigns... and His Son!"

The three gallant knights charged full speed into the wall of gruesome warriors and did not faint in their attack. It seemed a futile attempt, for these were massive men of war with no code to guide their wretched fight. The clash of armor and swords filled the forest amid the rising mist of the evening. Atop their steeds, the odds were slightly better since it was difficult for the Shadow Warriors to engage them more than one or two at a time. Triumph gave Gavinaugh a quick advantage over his first foe, and his sword felled that warrior quickly, but there were too many to overcome.

Gavinaugh heard Sandon grunt and saw the sword of one warrior tear through his left shoulder. He recovered and defended, but it was only a matter of time before their wounds would become fatal. Weston brought his sword to bear on one that greatly challenged him, and he too found an opening, causing his opponent to hit the ground with a thud. The Shadow Warriors intensified their attack, and Gavinaugh wondered if all would end here in the Black Woods this dreadful night.

Just then, fresh sounds of thundering steeds fell upon Gavinaugh's ears, but he dared not look to see to whom they belonged. The leader of the Shadow Warriors yelled a command, and the warriors on the fringes of the fray disengaged to meet the approaching men. It was enough to bring Gavinaugh and his men hope, for they soon heard the clash of metal just off to their left. The two battles raged, and Gavinaugh glanced toward the new fracas to discover the identity of their help. Embroiled in a vicious battle of their own were his friend Porunth and six fellow Silent Warriors. Their mighty forms brought new strength to the battle as the brilliant swords of the Prince flew to vanquish these ancient enemies of the King. Porunth worked his way to Gavinaugh, and they spoke in the throes of the fight.

"Gavinaugh, you must disengage and find Keanna!" he yelled above the battle sounds.

"But you are outnumbered," Gavinaugh called back.

"I know of this Devinoux and his stronghold. You cannot spare a moment," Porunth said and then thwarted the slice of a Shadow Warrior. Gavinaugh became preoccupied with his own battle until Porunth could speak again.

"Where do I look?" Gavinaugh asked.

"Follow the western edge of the forest to the swamplands. In the midst is his stronghold—a dragon known as the Tarmuwth guards the entrance. You must be ready!" Porunth shouted and deflected another blow. "Take my shield. You will need it to defeat the dragon."

Porunth executed a powerful blow that stunned his opponent long enough for him to engage the warrior Gavinaugh was against. Then Porunth threw his shield to Gavinaugh and drew his short blade with his left hand.

Gavinaugh paused for a moment—he could hardly leave his comrades to such a battle, but the urgency of his interrupted pursuit once again overcame him.

"Go!" Porunth yelled, and Gavinaugh pressed Triumph into a full gallop away from the battle.

Too much time had passed for him to hope to gain sight of Keanna and the Shadow Warrior, but Triumph did not hesitate in discovering their route. Gavinaugh rode for a good distance, and the evening turned to night. With daylight gone, Triumph slowed some. They followed the western edge of the Black Woods until they eventually came to the swamplands. Here the forest turned to moss and mud. Standing water generated a thick, low-lying fog that completely covered the ground, making navigation impossible for all except a Kasian horse like Triumph, able to guide where ordinary horses could not. The solid ground was impossible for Gavinaugh to see, and he was grateful for Triumph's special abilities. He let the steed focus on the hidden terrain beneath the fog and trusted the course to the animal. His progress now was slow, and Gavinaugh forced himself to be still. He looked ahead across the swamp and saw the faint outline of an eerie abode.

As Triumph brought him closer, Gavinaugh's muscles began to tense. In the midst of the swamp, the marshy mud and water yielded to an island of hard, dark soil. Black spires of an unusual substance protruded up from the ground to form a ghostly castle of evil. Some of the spires towered high above. An occasional pool of a black substance was aflame and gave a flickering orange glow to the surroundings. The stronghold of Devinoux was a ghastly place.

Just short of the embankment, Triumph stopped as a wicked raspy sound emanating from the stronghold rumbled across the swamp. *That hideous sound must come from the Tarmuwth,* Gavinaugh thought.

He coaxed Triumph to take him the remaining distance to the embankment of the stronghold and dismounted. Gavinaugh saw faint tracks in the hard ground. He drew his sword and tightened his grip on Porunth's shield. Though his right arm was weak, he was able to bear the shield adequately. Triumph was content to stay on the edge of the embankment as Gavinaugh proceeded into the stronghold and into the lair of the Tarmuwth. A wall of closely spaced black spires formed the boundary of the stronghold. Gavinaugh found an opening and cautiously entered.

The dancing shadows caused by the flames and spires occasionally startled Gavinaugh into thinking he saw movement behind him. He proceeded farther into the heart of the stronghold, searching the eerie landscape for some sign of Keanna. The smell of rotting flesh became stronger with each step he took. He maneuvered around one large stone spire, and something white fluttered to his right. He drew back his sword to strike and then realized that a fragment of Keanna's dress hung from the jagged tip of a smaller spire. He reached for the torn material, and it burst into flames. Gavinaugh instantly recoiled and held up his shield to deflect what he realized was an expulsion of flame from some hideous creature.

He crouched behind the protection of his shield and a large spire. Without his full suit of armor, he was vulnerable. He was thankful that only the hairs on the back of his arm had been singed. The flame had only lasted a moment and was immediately followed by a screech from the throat of the dragon. The near-deafening sound reverberated throughout the lair. The high pitch hurt Gavinaugh's ears, and he heard Triumph whinny in pain in the distance. He took the opportunity to see what monster he was facing. It was enough to shake his courage and test the mettle of his heart.

The creature looked like something straight from the Isle of Sedah. Its head was triangular, with two long horns protruding above its eyes back toward its spine. A shorter horn rose from the crest of its nose and arched rearward as well. Long, sharp teeth protruded from its upper and lower jaws. Its neck was slightly longer than a horse's, and its body was scaled like a snake's. It walked on all four legs but stood on its hind two to strike at its prey and to breathe fire. The hind legs were powerful, with large talons that gripped the ground for leverage, and the forelimbs were nearly as strong, but the talons here were longer and sharper. A connecting skin ran from the forelimbs to partway down the body. When the beast rose up, it seemed to double in size as it spread its limbs apart. The tail ended in a spade with numerous sharp horns that flicked left and right as it walked and hunted.

Gavinaugh retreated behind a spire and took a deep breath. The Tarmuwth stood taller than he and looked to weigh four times as much. It was an ominous sight. Only now did he realize that the ground around him was scattered with fragments of half-eaten bones. The thought of

Keanna in this place gave him great anguish, and his only thought was to free her from such an evil prison...if she was still alive.

Gavinaugh dodged behind different spires, hoping the creature would lose track of him. He began to circle about the beast and wondered at its capability to see and smell. He found a vantage point and watched as the creature licked at the air with its forked tongue, smelling for its prey. It screeched again, and Gavinaugh tried to cover his ears. He was breathing so hard that he took a moment to settle himself. He surveyed the area to plot his next course, and just as he was about to sprint to the next spire, he spotted a clearing in the distance. On the far side was a tattered figure in white held by thick ropes to a massive towering spire.

Gavinaugh knew that Devinoux must be near. He silently maneuvered farther away from the Tarmuwth and slowly made his way behind the spire Keanna was tied to. After each movement he waited and listened. He cautiously crept to the front of the spire. When Keanna caught her first glimpse of him, she inhaled in quiet exclamation.

"Gavinaugh!" she whispered. Her voice conveyed a sense of renewed hope, and the sound of it strengthened his heart. He sheathed his sword and drew his long-knife. Her arms were stretched wide and held in place by a rope tied to iron anchors high in the spire.

"Where is he?" Gavinaugh asked as he cut one of the ropes holding her arms.

"I'm not sure. He's not far, though. He—*Gavinaugh!*" she yelled as a sword screamed toward his head. He dropped the knife, turned, and brought his strong arm to the shield to bear the force of Devinoux's sword. Gavinaugh was off balance, and the blow sent him reeling to the ground. Devinoux covered him immediately and brought another cut on him from above. Gavinaugh deflected again with the shield and was able to draw his sword.

With one arm free, Keanna reached up to untie her other arm, but the knot was too tight to loosen with only one hand. She reached for the knife that lay at her feet, but it was just beyond her reach. She strained at the rope that still held her arm and could barely touch the hilt of the knife with her free hand. A horrific screech filled the air as the Tarmuwth dragon became aware of the ruckus.

Gavinaugh thwarted two more slices from Devinoux, and the warrior cursed as Gavinaugh regained his feet and took a defensive posture. The Shadow Warrior paused in his attack. He swung his sword from side to side as if to taunt Gavinaugh. Here in his stronghold, Devinoux looked even mightier than before. A mass of rippling muscles encased his frame from neck to feet. But it was the dark, steely eyes that unnerved Gavinaugh the most. They were windows into the soul of a monster. When he had faced Devinoux's sword before, Gavinaugh was his plaything. He wondered if the training of the Prince had truly elevated his level of mastery enough to be able to contend with such a powerful and evil foe.

"I knew you would play the fool and come for her. Here in my domain no one will come to save you. Now I will finish what I started years ago!" The Shadow Warrior's voice was full of hatred and loathing. "The Prince thinks He has made a knight of you, but I see in your eyes that you are but a cowardly knave. And this wench you are trying to save is nothing more than a slave for me and meat for my dragon." He laughed loudly and with such arrogance that Gavinaugh felt the anger rise within him.

"By the name of the Prince I bear this sword! By His strength and His might, you will fall this day!" Gavinaugh proclaimed and attacked the Shadow Warrior with the might of the Prince. Their swords flew with the speed of lightning and exploded with the sound of thunder as each countered and attacked time after time. Gavinaugh saw alarm momentarily cross his adversary's face.

Another screech blasted through the air—much closer this time.

Devinoux was a formidable foe, one of Lucius's top warriors. Gavinaugh did not underestimate his skill or his ruthlessness, for he had discerned what kind of warrior he was. The fight raged on and the dragon came closer. Gavinaugh felt the walls of defeat closing in upon him. The swords flashed again and Devinoux withdrew slightly. He lowered his sword and began to laugh. Gavinaugh wondered at his response until he heard the terrifying screech of the Tarmuwth just behind him.

Gavinaugh was now caught between the deadly sword of a mighty Shadow Warrior and the ripping claws of a fire-breathing dragon. He looked back at Devinoux, whose laughter suddenly became a gasp. Devinoux's eyes grew wide, and his face reddened in fury. As Devinoux turned to face a new foe, Gavinaugh saw that his own long-knife was protruding from the warrior's back. Devinoux raised his sword to strike at his assailant, but Gavinaugh seized the moment and plunged his sword deep into the warrior's chest. Devinoux fell to his knees, clutching at the knife that protruded from his back. Keanna stood behind him.

"I will never be your slave again. I belong to the Prince!" she said, and the warrior fell to the ground dead.

Gavinaugh turned to see the Tarmuwth rise up on its hind legs and spread its front limbs wide. In this position, the beast was a picture of absolute terror, and it took all Gavinaugh had not to collapse in fear. The stomach of the dragon convulsed, and Gavinaugh dove toward Keanna. He pulled her to the ground and sheltered her with the shield at the last instant before they were engulfed in a furnace of flames. The fringes of Keanna's dress caught fire, but there was little time to tend to it until they found cover. As soon as the encompassing flame was gone,

Gavinaugh grabbed Keanna's hand, and they ran to a nearby spire, where they extinguished her dress. Gavinaugh looked back at the Tarmuwth and saw that the body of the Shadow Warrior was aflame. The smell of burning flesh began to permeate the area. The dragon was coming toward them.

Gavinaugh leaned against the coarse texture of the spire and wondered how he could possibly save Keanna from such a beast. He took a moment to look at her and was amazed, for in spite of the terror, he saw new life in her eyes. He cocked his head slightly to one side as he wondered at the transformation.

"He found me, Gavinaugh. In the depths of this wretched place, He found me. My heart belongs to the Prince—and to you!" She kissed his cheek.

Just then the Tarmuwth shrieked. It was only a moment before it would be upon them. Gavinaugh had faced the blades of hundreds of men, but this was different, and he worried that he might fail Keanna here in the beginning moments of her newfound life.

He heard the guttural growls of the beast just on the far side of the spire.

"I need to get behind it somehow," he said.

"Give me the shield," she said and began to take it from him.

"What are you doing?"

"I am giving you the opportunity to save me, my brave knight," she said. With that, she darted into the open with the shield before he could stop her. She yelled at the Tarmuwth, and Gavinaugh's heart sank into his stomach. The dragon came to her on all fours, then raised itself up to strike. Gavinaugh quickly circled around the spire and advanced on the dragon from the rear. The beast convulsed, and Gavinaugh drew back his sword beneath the outstretched forelimb of the creature. He called upon every ounce of his strength as he executed a slice that tore into the belly of the Tarmuwth.

The flame that had expelled from its mouth toward Keanna was cut short as it screeched in pain. The large talons struck wildly at Gavinaugh, and one slashed across his thigh. Gavinaugh rolled away in gut-wrenching pain. The creature lowered itself to all fours. The beast's tail pounded down into the ground near where he lay, and Gavinaugh continued his roll to avoid its deadly spikes. Keanna ran to Gavinaugh and covered him with the shield just as the spade-shaped tail smashed into them. The shield flew from her arms and left them exposed to the dying thrashes of the injured dragon. The creature snapped at them with its powerful jaws, and Gavinaugh swiped back with his sword. Gavinaugh pushed Keanna away from the beast. He could barely stand because of the wound to his leg, but he tried to ready himself to strike again.

The tail swung once more at Gavinaugh. He ducked, but it was not enough. One of the spikes pierced deep into his side, and the impact sent him reeling toward a towering spire. His body slammed against its jagged edges, and he lost his grip on his sword. He nearly faded out of consciousness from the impact. The dragon writhed in pain but made its way toward Gavinaugh for the final kill. Keanna tried to come to him, but the wrathful beast was between them, and its tail was still whipping through the air. She looked for a weapon and saw the long-knife protruding from the burnt corpse of the Shadow Warrior. She ran and grabbed it.

Gavinaugh fought against the pain and searched for his sword as the dragon descended on him. Just as the Tarmuwth opened its jaws wide to crush him between its teeth, he found the hilt of his sword. The pain in his side was more than he could bear, but he knew that if he failed, Keanna would also die in the jaws of the dragon. He yelled and lunged at the heart of the beast with all his might, the tip of his sword leading the way. His sword plunged deep into the creature and found its mark. One final terrifying shriek emanated from the throat of the Tarmuwth. A moment later it fell to the ground on its side and became still in death.

Gavinaugh collapsed, and Keanna came to him. Her eyes revealed her great concern. She used the knife to cut long pieces of cloth from her dress and tightly bandaged his side and the gash in his leg. But his blood quickly soaked through the bandage, and the severity of the wound was clear—Gavinaugh was struggling to breathe. Her efforts seemed futile.

He reached up and touched her soiled cheek. "I...love you, Keanna," he said softly.

Tears welled up in her eyes as the gravity of the moment crushed down on her. "I love you, Gavinaugh. You can't leave me!"

She brought her face close to his.

"My sword," he whispered and then coughed. He grimaced at the pain.

Keanna ran to the body of the Tarmuwth and withdrew his sword. She brought it to him and held the hilt of the sword so he could see it, but he wrapped his hand about hers.

"Now...you must...carry the sword," he said with great difficulty.

Tears flowed freely down her cheeks. "Together, Gavinaugh...together we will carry the sword."

He managed a weak smile. "The Prince will be with you." His hand began to loosen about hers.

"No, Gavinaugh... *No!*"

Keanna's head jerked as she heard men approaching, and soon Weston and Sandon were beside her.

"Help him, please, help him," she pleaded.

At Porunth's command they had detached from the battle to come to Gavinaugh's aid. They looked at his wound, and their faces revealed their fear.

"Sandon, my pack," Weston said, and Sandon quickly went to retrieve it. He put fresh bandages over Keanna's, but the blood continued to flow freely. There seemed little he could do, and Gavinaugh slipped closer to the pit of death.

"Gavinaugh!" Weston called, but his words were interrupted by the quick approach of another rider. A large cloaked warrior on a white horse was making his way through the spires to their position. He dismounted and came to them.

"The battle is over, and Porunth has sent me to help," he said in a deep voice. Weston moved aside to allow the warrior access to Gavinaugh. Keanna looked hopefully into his eyes. The warrior reached beneath his cloak and produced a flask.

"He must drink this," he said and brought the flask to Gavinaugh's lips.

Keanna grabbed the long-knife and slashed across the flask and the hand of the warrior. The flask spilled to the ground, along with the blood from the warrior's gash. He recoiled and screamed in pain as he backed away.

"What are you doing, Keanna?" Weston shouted.

The warrior looked at her with fury in his eyes and reached for his sword.

Keanna stood up and pointed the knife at him.

"I have served under enough masters to know the good ones from the evil. Get away from him!" she yelled and drew back Gavinaugh's sword.

The Shadow Warrior cursed and drew his sword. "Fools! I will spill the blood of you all!"

Weston and Sandon drew their swords and positioned themselves between the warrior and Keanna.

"Leave, or the only blood spilled will be your own!" Weston said.

Suddenly, the sound of many horses began to filter through the spires of the dragon's lair. The Shadow Warrior cursed again. He quickly mounted his horse and departed. A moment later the clearing was filled with a dozen massive warriors. Porunth dismounted and came to Gavinaugh. Keanna knelt down opposite the warrior.

"Gavinaugh," Porunth said.

Gavinaugh opened his eyes and tried to speak but couldn't. Porunth motioned to one of his men, and he brought a pack to him. Together they tended to Gavinaugh's wounds and gave him water to drink. Porunth applied sweet salve to his wounds and dressed them with fresh bandages.

There in the eerie shadows of the Tarmuwth's lair, the Silent Warriors encircled the hero of the Outdwellers and watched him fight for every breath and for every beat of his heart. The moments passed, and Gavinaugh slipped in and out of consciousness. Keanna squeezed his hand and would not let it go. Porunth held a small vial to Gavinaugh's lips and carefully poured its contents into his mouth.

"He will not make it here," he said quietly and then looked at Keanna.

"No…no! Don't take him from me," she pleaded.

"He will die, Keanna."

She looked at Porunth and then at Gavinaugh.

She knelt down and kissed him. Although the anguish in her heart was obvious, she eventually released him to Porunth to save his life. "I shall never love another," she said, and her tears spilled onto Gavinaugh's cheeks.

Weston placed his arm around Keanna's shoulders. He lifted her up, and the Silent Warriors carried Gavinaugh away.

The sorrow of that night hung thicker than the fogs of Moorue about the hearts of his companions, and Keanna seemed as though part of her had died.

CHAPTER SIXTEEN

KINDRED QUESTS

 Keanna, Weston, and Sandon rode in silence back to Namor, for they were not prepared to begin the long journey back to Chessington and Cresthaven. They arrived at Captain Dante's estate late on the third day. Dante greeted them joyfully, but there was no joy in their hearts. They told him of Gavinaugh's demise, and he mourned greatly with them.

After four days of rest and preparation, they rose up to depart Namor for Cresthaven.

On the morning of their departure, they sat to eat a final meal with Dante. Although there were various attempts to lift the cloud of oppression during breakfast, the sadness upon each of their faces was impossible to hide. Midway through the meal, a servant came to Dante and whispered in his ear.

"Very good, thank you," Dante said and dismissed the servant before turning to the others. "It seems that a visitor from Chessington has just arrived and would like to see you before you depart," Captain Dante announced to the sober trio. "He claims to have known Gavinaugh."

They wondered if perhaps William or Cedric had come to visit them and the haven there. Dante brought them to a room in his manor where they were greeted at the door by a large fellow who was blocking their entrance to the room.

"It seems Sir Gavinaugh is more headstrong than I realized," Porunth said as he stepped aside. Gavinaugh was lying on a bed and carefully raised himself up on his elbow and smiled broadly.

"Gavinaugh!" Keanna screamed and ran to him. She embraced him, and he winced in pain, but it was soon replaced by a broad smile that expressed his joy. She sat on the bed next to him.

"It is good to see you, princess," he said.

"I can't believe it is really you." Her smile filled the room with radiance.

Weston and Sandon approached, and both seemed as giddy as schoolboys. Weston put his hand on Gavinaugh's shoulder as if to convince himself that he was real.

"What happened?" Sandon asked and looked at Porunth.

"During the days when we were preparing to ready our ship and take him across the sea, he recovered enough to refuse the voyage, in spite of the fact that he might still be in great danger." Porunth walked over to them and became very serious. He looked at Gavinaugh, a bit perturbed, and then turned to the others. "He will not fully recover here. He could collapse at any time. It is foolish to leave him, but his mind seems to be set." He looked at Keanna and raised one eyebrow, but she didn't see it for she had not taken her eyes from Gavinaugh.

"I am sure that my leaving him here will cause me no small amount of grief, but since I have come to know him, I have grown accustomed to that!" Porunth said as he walked over to Gavinaugh. He held out his arm and Gavinaugh took it.

"We are grateful to you and your men," Gavinaugh said as he looked up at his large friend.

"And the kingdom is grateful to you," Porunth said in return. He gave a flask and some salve to Keanna. "Make him drink this, and apply the salve to his wounds each day until it is gone."

"I will," she said.

Porunth turned and walked to the doorway. "Gentlemen, it is time for me to depart." He looked at his Arrethtraen friends and smiled. "It is a time of the Outdwellers. The Prince needs knights brave and bold to carry His words to the far reaches of the kingdom. Keep your swords sharp, and remember…we are always here, fighting with you side by side. Whether you see us or not, we are always here."

With that, Porunth exited the room and disappeared into the secret world of the Silent Warriors.

Gavinaugh's recovery was slow, but he was fueled by the realization that his mission to train and equip his fellow knights was not yet fulfilled. If his days in Arrethtrae were to be cut short, he wanted first to be sure that the havens were ready to stand by themselves. He also did not deny that his heart could hardly bear the thought of Keanna dealing once again with the death of someone for whom she cared so deeply. He had spent many months trying to share the compassion of the Prince with her and win her forgiveness. In the beginning days of her new life as a Knight of the Prince, he could not abandon her, no matter the cost. He decided that the risk of dying from his wounds was not enough to nullify the joy of living even a short time with the affections of Keanna.

In time, Gavinaugh began to diligently train Keanna in the art of the sword, and her heart waxed strong in the ways of the Prince and of the Code. She became a mighty knight, who stood beside him and the other knights as they continued the mission given them by the Prince.

Gavinaugh, Keanna, Weston, and Sandon journeyed onward.

Before them lay the vast regions of a grand kingdom, and they had been called to go. It was a time to rise up and be strong—a time to honor the King and His Son. Gavinaugh felt the hearts of many people calling out for a Deliverer, and he had purposed in his heart to answer them with the only name that could ever bring them hope and new life—the Prince!

FINAL
DAWN

Alas, the tale of Sir Gavinaugh and his valiant quest to reach the kingdom of Arrethtrae for the King and the Prince is told. I, Cedric of Chessington, count it a great honor to have known the heart of such a brave and courageous knight. The fame of the gallant Sir Gavinaugh went forth throughout the entire kingdom, and he is considered a champion for the Prince, for his sword flew forth to destroy the strongholds of many Shadow Warriors. Through his quest, many people were gathered to the Prince.

I tell the story of Sir Gavinaugh, not to bring glory to him, but to inspire others to rise up and put on the armor of the King…to cross the barren lands of the kingdom with hope and joy in the One who sacrificed Himself to save many, to bring the power of the Prince against the strongholds of the Dark Knight that imprison the souls of men. All who hear are called. All who are called are able.

It is now time for me to cease the telling and prepare for the battle that is coming. But perhaps before I go, you might care to know what ultimately happened to the mighty Sir Gavinaugh and the fair Lady Keanna. It is said that their love for each other grew to transcend the highest mountains of Arrethtrae. Their marriage was as simple as a peasant's but seemed as royal as a king's—for their hearts needed nothing more than each other and the Prince. Unfortunately, not long after their union, Gavinaugh's wounds from the Tarmuwth dragon eventually overcame him during one of his battles with a Shadow Warrior, and he was carried away across the Great Sea by the Silent Warriors. Keanna's grief was so great that the entire kingdom could feel the pain within her heart. But she rose up and carried on the work Gavinaugh had begun. As for the saga of the rest of their lives, I am afraid I cannot tell it, for such a man and woman as these deserve the eloquent words of a herald far better than I.

The time of my departure is here. Place your hand gently on the soil beside my own, and feel the rumble of the earth beneath. The power of a thousand thousands is coming…evil warriors fighting against the Noble One. Here I stand with Him. Take up your sword and come with me, for the Prince is calling. And if you do not go…who will?

DISCUSSION QUESTIONS

To further facilitate the understanding of the biblical allegory of this series, a few discussion questions and answers are provided below.

CHAPTER 1

1. Throughout the first chapter, Gavinaugh slowly realizes what his mission from the Prince entails. What is that mission?
2. The Outdwellers are people of Arrethtrae who are not citizens of Chessington. Who do they represent?
3. Porunth, a Silent Warrior, tells Gavinaugh that it is "easy to tell when one has been with Him." We should live so it is easy for others to see that Christ lives in us as well. Find a verse that talks about this.
4. When Gavinaugh first meets two Knights of the Prince, they fear that he has come to arrest them. They even call him the "Tyrant of Chessington." Then Weston comes and proclaims that Gavinaugh is a true Knight of the Prince. What does this event portray, and who is Weston?
5. Gavinaugh tells William and Barrett that "the Prince has made all things new" in him. Find a verse that supports this statement.

CHAPTER 2

1. In the first paragraph of this chapter, there was a disagreement among the Knights of the Prince regarding the Outdwellers and what they must do to become true Knights of the Prince. Find the passage in Acts where the disciples had a similar disagreement regarding the Gentiles.
2. Until this point, Weston represented Barnabas. However, his biblical representation broadens. Who does he become now?

3. What does the conversation between Gavinaugh and Cade represent? Find verses in the Bible that are discussed in this passage.

CHAPTER 3

1. Gavinaugh confronts the Shadow Warrior who is terrorizing Kumbria. His moving words speak of the power of the Prince. What event in Acts does this represent?

CHAPTER 4

1. What does Santiok represent?
2. Weston tries to pacify Gavinaugh's intense anger over the despicable treatment of people by saying, "They do not know the ways of the Prince. They have lived in this darkened condition since the beginning of the kingdom." Paul states something similar in chapter five of the book of Ephesians about living in a darkened condition. Can you find the verse?
3. Gavinaugh addresses the people of Santiok in order to share the words of the Prince with them, and at the end of his address, Gavinaugh pleads, "Free your slaves and show compassion to your fellow citizens, as the King has shown His compassion to you." The people's obnoxious response prompts Gavinaugh and Weston to leave the auction. Find three parallel events in Acts 13.
4. At one point, Gavinaugh tells the men that to become Knights of the Prince they must "Simply believe, tell others, and prepare." What does this represent?

CHAPTER 5

1. Keanna has been an active character for the past few chapters. Now do you know who she represents?

2. Gavinaugh abandoned Keanna when the Shadow Warriors first came for her. Now he has chosen to protect her. What does this change of heart portray?

3. Have you ever held a grudge against someone? What helped you overcome your anger? Find a verse that addresses anger.

CHAPTER 6

1. Who does Sandon represent?

2. After Gavinaugh loses consciousness from the brutal beating, he has an encounter with the Prince, who encourages Gavinaugh to continue with his mission. What does this represent?

3. What event in Paul's life does Gavinaugh's beating symbolize?

CHAPTER 7

1. Although Gavinaugh remains at Penwell, the biblical location of his mission moves somewhere else. Where is this place in the Bible?

2. Gavinaugh is again arrested and thrown into Penwell's prison. What does this represent?

3. After spending many days and nights in prison, Gavinaugh, Weston, and Sandon are released when two Silent Warriors appear and order the governor to release his three prisoners. What does this event allegorize?

4. At the end of this chapter, Sandon asks to travel with Gavinaugh and Weston. What does this represent?

CHAPTER 8

1. The beginning of this chapter recounts the journey from Penwell to Thecia. Read Acts 17:1–14. Have you ever found yourself the target of ridicule or harsh treatment because you believe in Jesus?

2. What does the city of Thecia represent?

3. What do you think the Court of the Lords represents?

4. Gavinaugh tells his fellow knights that to the Thecians he will be a Thecian so he can win their attention and tell them of the Prince. Find the passage written by Paul in 1 Corinthians concerning this. Why do you think this is important?

5. The Thecian nobility have devoted all their time, energy, and wealth to attaining new heights of nobility through their grand tournaments. What does this cultural development symbolize?

CHAPTER 9

1. What does the Tournament of Lords represent?

CHAPTER 10

1. At the beginning of this chapter, Weston warns Gavinaugh not to go back to Chessington. Find in the chapter in Acts where Paul's fellow disciples warn him not to return to Jerusalem. What is Paul's response?

2. Gavinaugh journeys to Chessington and is captured and imprisoned. Leisel visits him and pleads for his love one last time. Who do you think Leisel represents?

3. Leisel is described as "a prisoner behind the bars of religious devotion to a false concept of nobility." What do you think this means?

4. In the New Testament, Paul warns believers not to fall back into the bondage of the Law. When this happens, our faith becomes empty because our relationship with God becomes burdensome and not joyful. Is your relationship with God burdensome or joyful? If burdensome, why and what can you do to change it?

CHAPTER 11

1. In this chapter, Kifus begins to represent more than just the head of the Pharisees. He questions Gavinaugh about his motives. Who else does Kifus represent in this scene?

2. At one point during Gavinaugh's explanation of his motives, Kifus seems to understand the truth and becomes afraid. Yet he does not become a follower. Why do you think this is? Is understanding the truth enough to become saved? Why or why not?

3. Gavinaugh is eventually sent on a ship to the Namorian realm. Who do the Namorians represent?

CHAPTER 12

1. Read Acts 27. The Tempests attack the *Raven,* and the crew is fearful. What do the Tempests represent?

2. Gavinaugh uses his sword to help save the crew of the *Raven* from being captured by the Tempests. What does this symbolize, and what verse in Acts 27 applies here?

3. We often encounter "storms" in our lives. What lesson can we learn from Paul in facing our storms? Find a Scripture verse to support your answer.

CHAPTER 13

1. What island in Acts is represented by the Isles of Melogne?

2. In the scene with the strangler vine, Gavinaugh survives because of the sword training he received from the Prince. Through the sword he was protected. How does this relate to Paul's survival of the poisonous snakebite?

3. On the island, Pliubus's father is taken captive by Lord Malthos. What does this represent, and who is Lord Malthos?

4. Gavinaugh defeats Lord Malthos and frees all of his slaves. What does this symbolize?

Chapter 14

1. Gavinaugh continues to court Keanna and win her heart. What does this represent?

2. Gavinaugh loves Keanna but realizes that she must belong to the Prince before he can fully give his heart to her. Have you ever been tempted to compromise your convictions to please someone else instead of God?

3. Keanna finds it difficult to believe in the Prince because of the pain she has experienced as well as the pain she sees all around her. Find the verse that tells us to be ready to give an answer to those who are seeking God.

4. In Keanna's moment of decision to follow the Prince, the Shadow Warriors steal her away. Find a parable in Matthew where Jesus talks about how this can happen to someone who hears the word of the kingdom.

Chapter 15

1. Keanna is taken to Devinoux's stronghold, which is the lair of the Tarmuwth, where Gavinaugh must face the dragon. What do you think the dragon represents?

2. There are many ways that Satan can establish a stronghold in our lives. How does Gavinaugh defeat this stronghold, and what can we learn from his battle? Find a verse to support your answer.

3. Keanna frees herself and helps Gavinaugh defeat Devinoux and the dragon. Why do you think she finds courage to do this, and how does this apply to a Christian's life? Can you find a verse that supports your answer?

4. A Shadow Warrior poses as a Silent Warrior and tries to kill Gavinaugh. What does the Bible have to say about this kind of demonic deception? How can we be as discerning as Keanna?

CHAPTER 16

1. When Gavinaugh is wounded by the dragon, he nearly dies. He is eventually taken across the Great Sea because of his wounds, and Keanna continues his work. What does this represent biblically?

ANSWERS TO
DISCUSSION QUESTIONS

CHAPTER 1

1. The Prince charged Gavinaugh to share His message with and train the Outdwellers.

2. In a broad sense, they represent all non-Jewish people of the world, the Gentiles. Later in the book, Outdwellers are specifically represented by one character. Watch for who this might be.

3. Matthew 5:16.

4. When the disciples feared that Saul would imprison them but Barnabas vouched for Saul's sincerity in Acts 9:26–27. Weston represents Barnabas.

5. 2 Corinthians 5:17.

CHAPTER 2

1. Acts 15:1–2, 5–19.

2. Weston now represents any of the disciples who traveled with Paul, be it Barnabas, Silas, Luke, or someone else. (Acts 15:22).

3. Biblical truths as taught by Jesus and Paul (Mark 10:25; Matthew 6:19–20; Luke 14:16–23; Revelation 5:10; Romans 10:8–9).

CHAPTER 3

1. All of chapter 3 represents Paul and Barnabas's missionary journey to the city of Paphos on the isle of Cyprus, where Paul blinds a sorcerer and converts the proconsul of the country in Acts 13:6–13.

CHAPTER 4

1. Santiok represents Antioch (Acts 13:14).
2. Ephesians 5:8.
3. Paul's sermon in Acts 13:16–41, Paul and Barnabas's charge in verses 46–47, and their departure in verse 50.
4. These are essentially the words of the Great Commission, given by Jesus to His disciples. The remark in the book represents Paul's dedication to Jesus and His teaching.

CHAPTER 5

1. Keanna represents the Gentiles.
2. Gavinaugh has learned through the Prince that the Outdwellers are also called to become Knights of the Prince. This is allegorical of Paul's outreach to the Gentiles.
3. Answer based on personal experience; one choice is Ephesians 4:26.

CHAPTER 6

1. Timothy (Acts 16:1–3).
2. The appearance of Jesus to Paul to encourage him in Acts 18:9–10.
3. The stoning of Paul at Lystra in Acts 14:19–20.

CHAPTER 7

1. By now, Paul has traveled to Philippi in Acts 16:12.
2. Paul's imprisonment at Philippi (he was thrown into prison because he cast out a demon of divination in a servant girl in Acts 16:16–24).
3. God's intervention to free Paul and Silas through the dramatic event of an earthquake (Acts 16:25–26).
4. Timothy traveling with Paul (Acts 16:4).

CHAPTER 8

1. Answer based on personal experience.
2. Athens, Greece (Acts 17:15).
3. The Athenians' Mars Hill, where there were altars to many gods including "the unknown god" (Acts 17:23).
4. 1 Corinthians 9:22–23. At this point in Christianity's history, the gospel of Jesus Christ was just being introduced to many cultures. Without compromising righteousness, Paul adapted to each culture to establish credibility so he could tell others about Jesus.
5. The Athenian pursuit of wisdom and understanding through intellectual and scholarly debates (Acts 17:21.) Just as the Athenians use their words—the Thecians' swords of nobility)—Paul uses the Word of God—Gavinaugh's sword of the Prince (Hebrews 4:12).

CHAPTER 9

1. The entire biblical event when Paul disputed in the synagogue and the marketplace, including when the prominent philosophers brought him to them to discuss his "new doctrine" (Acts 17:16–34).

CHAPTER 10

1. Acts 21:4, 11–12. Paul says that he is ready to die at Jerusalem for Jesus' sake.
2. Leisel represents the Jewish people just as Keanna represents the Gentiles.
3. "False concept of nobility" symbolizes a faith built on one's works and the law for salvation instead of on simple faith in Jesus Christ.
4. Answer based on personal experience. Read 1 Thessalonians 5:16–18.

CHAPTER 11

1. Kifus represents other leaders in Jerusalem at the time of Paul's captivity, specifically Governors Felix and Festus, and King Agrippa, as found in Acts 24–26.

2. Kifus might have understood the truth, but he realized that he would have to give up everything in order to become a follower of the Prince. His selfishness and pride kept him from submitting to the truth. Understanding the truth is not enough. Jesus requires us to give Him lordship of our lives as well. James 2:19 says, "You believe that there is one God. You do well. Even the demons believe—and tremble!"

3. The Romans.

CHAPTER 12

1. The mighty storm that Paul's ship endured for many days.

2. The sword always represents God's Word, and in Acts 27:24, God sends an angel to Paul to tell him that he and the entire crew will make it through the storm.

3. Answer based on personal experience. One pertinent Bible verse is Hebrews 13:5: "I will never leave you nor forsake you."

CHAPTER 13

1. Malta in Acts 28:1.

2. God told Paul that he would make it safely to Rome because he was to give his testimony before Caesar. God's Word protected Paul from even a poisonous snakebite (Acts 28:3–6).

3. This represents when the father of Publius becomes ill (Acts 28:7–8). Lord Malthos represents disease and sickness. Malthos is derived from *malady* and *pathosis*.

4. Paul's healing of Publius's father and others who had diseases (Acts 28:8–9).

CHAPTER 14

1. Paul's fervent desire to see the Gentiles' hearts turn to Jesus Christ as their Lord and Savior.

2. Answer based on personal experience. Psalm 37:4 says, "Delight yourself also in the LORD, and He shall give you the desires of your heart." Often we must be patient, but remember that God is faithful and knows your heart.

3. 1 Peter 3:15: "But sanctify the Lord God in your hearts, and always be ready to give a defense to everyone who asks you a reason of the hope that is in you, with meekness and fear."

4. Matthew 13:3–23, the parable of the sower. Verse 19 says that the wicked one "snatches away what was sown in his heart."

CHAPTER 15

1. *Tarmuwth* is Hebrew for "deceit." Without the truth of Jesus Christ, the world is under the power of Satan's deception. Satan is often referred to as a dragon in the Bible.

2. Gavinaugh overcomes this stronghold by once again using the sword, God's Holy Word. It is powerful. Second Corinthians 10:3–4 says, "For though we walk in the flesh, we do not war according to the flesh. For the weapons of our warfare are not carnal but mighty in God for pulling down strongholds."

3. Keanna became confident and found courage to fight against her foes when she put her trust in the Prince and believed. As Christians, we receive our strength from the Lord and can do battle against the evil one. Psalm 31:24 says, "Be of good courage, and He shall strengthen your heart, all you who hope in the LORD."

4. The Bible says in 2 Corinthians 11:13–15 that Satan disguises himself as an angel of light to deceive people. A close relationship with the Lord through Bible study and prayer will allow the Holy Spirit to give us great spiritual discernment.

CHAPTER 16

1. Paul is eventually killed for his faith in Jesus Christ. The fruit of his work—the gospel being spread throughout the world by the Gentiles—continues through us today.

Ballad of the Prince

Written for Kingdom's Quest

Music and Lyrics by Emily Black
Edited by Brittney Black

1. O - ver the a - ges and a - cross man - y halls Songs of hon - or and val - or are sung But the
2. I was once a trai - tor But He set me free

song of the Prince Sur - pas-ses them all A bal-lad that's only begun In the
I was once a sla-ve To the en - e - my

heart of the des - ert He found a boy And made him a man To
I watched them kill Him He helped Him die

©2006 Emily Elizabeth Black

AUTHOR'S COMMENTARY

Kingdom's Quest was written as an attempt to capture the spiritual conflict and significance of Paul's life on this earth. As an instrument to bring the gospel of Jesus Christ to the Gentiles, Paul's ministry shook two worlds: the temporal and the spiritual. I brought the character of Keanna into the story as a primary point of focus for this spiritual drama.

Keanna represents the Gentile world that, until the time of Christ, seemed to have little regard for matters of spiritual truth, as evidenced by the attitude of God's chosen people toward them. This was depicted when Gavin refused to help Keanna as she was fleeing the Shadow Warriors near Cartelbrook. The Gentiles were, for the most part, subject to the powers of Satan and his demons until God told Peter and Paul to take the truth of Jesus to them.

As the gospel of Jesus spread into the world, His power began to invade Satan's realm of strongholds and set people free. Paul's fervent desire to see the world of the Gentiles saved is portrayed through the character of Gavinaugh and his growing love for Keanna. Keanna's character transitioned from enslavement to true freedom as she yielded to the truth of the Prince. Paul never married, but just as the Bible uses marriage symbolically to describe the relationship between the Father and Jews in the Old Testament, and the church and Jesus in the New Testament, with some trepidation I used the same symbol of marriage to portray Paul's love for the Gentiles. The culmination of the battle for the souls of the Gentiles occurs when the Shadow Warrior and the Tarmuwth dragon (*tarmuwth* is Hebrew for "deceit") attempt to enslave Keanna once again, but Gavinaugh gives his life to free her.

It is my heartfelt desire to honor the Lord Jesus Christ with all of my work here on earth. The purpose of this series is to draw people to Christ through parable stories that point them to the Scriptures. I used the example of Jesus for my guide, as He taught the people through many parables that drew the attention of His audience. My prayer for you is that your zeal for living for Jesus will grow and never be quenched by the cares of this world.

Being confident of this very thing, that He who has begun a good work in you will complete it until the day of Jesus Christ.

Philippians 1:6

Discover the ultimate battle between good and evil